Dear Me,

Mom just read my journal. Here is what I'm thinking:

#1—Nothing happened at Derrick's house, so I don't know what the big deal is.

#2—I can take care of myself, which was actually proven *in the journal.*

#3—What gives my mother the right to just go in my room and read my journal?

#4—If my mom keeps me from getting the car my daddy promised me, I will leave!

#5—Derrick does not look like Bow-Wow. Do not ever fall for a guy you've only seen from the ninth row up in the stands at a basketball game.

Maybe I should stop writing all of my personal stuff down. But if I do that, who will I tell all my problems? I mean, I have my friends, but they don't understand me like this journal does. No, I can't give up the journal. I'll just have to find a good hiding place for it.

—Karis I've-Been-Wronged Reed

Trouble in My Way

MICHELLE STIMPSON

POCKET BOOKS

NEW YORK   LONDON   TORONTO   SYDNEY

Pocket Books
A Division of Simon & Schuster, Inc.
1230 Avenue of the Americas
New York, NY 10020

First Pocket Books trade paperback edition November 2008

POCKET and colophon are registered trademarks of Simon & Schuster, Inc.

For information about special discounts for bulk purchases,
please contact Simon & Schuster Special Sales
at 1-800-456-6798 or business@simonandschuster.com.

Designed by Carla Jayne Little

Manufactured in the United States of America

10 9 8 7 6 5 4 3 2 1

Library of Congress Cataloging-in-Publication Data

Stimpson, Michelle.
    Trouble in my way / by Michelle Stimpson.
        p.   cm.
    Summary: Coming of age in Texas, sixteen-year-old Karis shares her thoughts in a series of diary entries.
    1. Coming of age—Fiction. 2. Mothers and daughters—Fiction. 3. African Americans—Fiction. 4. Christian life—Fiction. 5. Diaries—Fiction. I. Title.
    PZ7.S860135Tr 2008
    [Fic]—dc22
                                                                        2008021764

ISBN-13: 978-1-4165-8668-5
ISBN-10:   1-4165-8668-7

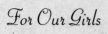

For Our Girls

Acknowledgments

First of all, I thank God from Whom all blessings flow. It's amazing how You set me up for this. Thanks also to my friends and family who always listen to my ideas and give me even more ideas from the drama that we all call life. Special thanks to my mom, Wilma J. Music. As I wrote this novel and thought of all my teenage antics, I realize now that you picked your battles with me. You picked the right ones. God handled the rest. Thanks, Dad (Michael), and to my brothers (Tony and Michael) also for bearing with your big sister.

Thanks to those who read the first draft in its entirety—Jayne Knighton and Ellen Kimbrough and Mrs. Kimbrough. Apparently, one can never have too many friends with a last name that begins with K. Special thanks, also, to Stephanie Yowell for giving me your youthful perspective. I am grateful for your stamp of approval. Thanks to all of my friends and supporters at Oak Cliff Bible Fellowship, Region 10 Education Service Center, and all the book clubs that show me much love.

I owe a great BIG thanks to ReShonda Tate Billingsley, who first encouraged me to write this young adult novel—over vanilla shakes, mind you. Your generosity of spirit is sincerely appreciated. A shout out to the Anointed Authors on Tour—Vanessa Miller, Kendra Norman-Bellamy, Tia McCollors, Dr. Vivi Monroe Congress, Shewanda Riley, and Norma Jarrett. Your sisterhood is priceless. And to my everyday sisters, Kim Scott, Jeanne Muldrew, and Shannon Green, thanks for all the love.

Thanks to my agent, Sara Camilli, for your expertise and guidance. I look forward to many more. Finally, thanks to Brigitte at Pocket Books.

God Bless!

chapter one

Dear Me,

Derrick is cute—NOT! I can't believe I risked my life by having Tamisha take me over to his house instead of the football game. Seriously, if my mom found out, I would be writing my eulogy instead of writing this journal entry. And for what? Some boy who does not have one single real DVD in his famed DVD collection! I swear, every single movie he had was bootleg. I think his whole room was bootleg. His whole game is bootleg, when I think about it! He acts like one thing in the beginning, but when you look closely, you realize it's not exactly as good as the real thing. Okay, here's what happened: Tamisha took me over to his house—we synchronized our watches—she was to pick me up in EXACTLY forty-five minutes. There was no one except Derrick at his house, so I knew I didn't want to be over there too long. Anyway, we started watching a movie on the floor in his bedroom. Everything was fine *at first. I mean, so long as I didn't stare at him right in the face, it was okay. I just kept trying to think about all the wonderful things we'd talked about on the phone because he was NOT as cute as I remember him. So, there we were watching the movie to the best of my ability since it was a little blurry. I was just getting beyond the fact that I had to ignore the line running through the middle of the screen, and the next thing I know, Derrick is trying to kiss and hug and all that. I was like, "Hold up! Wait a minute!" and he was like, "What's wrong, baby?" like this is some kind of bad music video. I could not believe how he was trying to turn our movie-watching into some kinda romantic rondayvu (spelling??). When we're on the phone, he's an innocent little boy, but when we were together, he was a grown octopus! I'm not saying I wasn't feeling his kisses— I'm just saying, I wasn't trying to do all that. See, I know how and when to draw the line. I know when enough is enough. Thank God, Tamisha came right on time! I was outta there so quick! I know Derrick is nice and all, but he is not the one for me. Maybe we should just be friends because #1, he is not that cute, and #2 he is having some issues right now that I cannot help him out with. I think I'll leave him alone until his hormones settle down.*

Karis Laying-Low Reed

I don't know which is more stupid—me going over to Derrick's house, or me writing about it in my journal knowing how straight-up nosey my mother is. I mean, I know that a momma's gotta do what a momma's gotta do. But does a momma *have* to read my journal and get all up in my personal business? What about my American rights? My Texas rights? My basic human need for privacy? First my journal—next thing you know, she'll be following me into the bathroom.

The bathroom; that's a good place to go right about now.

I wait until my mother turns her back and takes a breather between the yelling spells. I'm doing my best to rise from the couch without making a sound. Her head whips around instantly. "Where do you think you're going?"

"To the bathroom," I reply, throwing in a bit of whine for effect.

"Sidown," she hisses.

I bounce on the balls of my feet, faking the biological emergency. "But I've really gotta go."

She throws her hands up in the air and they land on her hips as she half-laughs, "*That's* what you should have been saying when Tamisha dropped you off at your little man-ish boyfriend's house when you were supposed to be at a football game: *'I've really gotta go.'* But noooo, you couldn't say it *then,* so don't be sayin' it *now.* You ain't really gotta go *nowhere.* Okay?"

I've already slipped back onto the couch, and I mumble, "Yes, ma'am."

My mother does a cha-cha slide over to me and pushes hot words onto my face. "I can't hear you!"

I look her in the eyes and answer again, "Yes, ma'am."

Then she takes a few steps back toward the center of our living room and reaches down to the coffee table, picking up my beloved pink-heart journal again. I still cannot believe she read it. "And what is this?" she traces over the entry until her pearl-tipped fingernail lands on what she's looking for. She wags her head as she mocks me, " 'When we're on the phone, he's an innocent little boy, but when we were together, he was a grown *octopus.*' What's that supposed to mean, huh?"

Mrs. Clawson, my pre-Advanced Placement English teacher, would have appreciated my fine use of figurative language. "It's just a metaphor, Mom."

"A meta-four!" She slams my journal shut, and the resulting puff of air makes her soft brown bangs do the wave. "According to this diary, it would have had a meta-*five* and a meta-*six*, given a few more minutes. Tell me, Karis, what would you have done if Tamisha hadn't come back to pick you up when she did, huh? What if Tamisha hadn't been on time? What if you had started 'feeling' your little boyfriend's kisses? Then what?"

I want to tell her that, first of all, Derrick is not my boyfriend. But somehow I think that might damage my case, so I keep that bit of information to myself. The second thing I wish I could tell her is that there was no way I would have done anything stupid with Derrick. I want to tell her that I timed things precisely to protect myself from crossing the line. I also want to tell her that Derrick and I talk on the phone for hours at a time and I have intense feelings for him. Next to Tamisha and Sydney, Derrick is my best friend, kind of. Well, I used to trust him until he turned into that eight-legged marine creature. Besides, he is really only a six on the face and body scale. When I saw him on the basketball court, he looked like Bow Wow. But when I saw him up close at his house, he looked like *maybe* he could be Bow Wow's half brother. Plus one of his front teeth was longer than the other. Believe me, my mother does not ever have to worry about me sneaking off to Derrick's house again.

Nonetheless, my mother would not understand these things. She's a minister. Need I say more? So in response to her question about what I would have done, I default to my standard answer, which turns out to be the stupidest thing I can say. "I don't know."

"You don't *know*? What you mean, you don't *know*? I betcha Derrick knows. I betcha Tamisha knows. *I* know what would have happened, 'cause it happened to me and that's how I ended up pregnant with you when I was your age. You think I don't know what boys and girls your age do when they're together for hours unsupervised? And, really, it don't take *hours*. It only takes a few minutes to do something that can change your life forever!"

She stands there for a minute, towering over me. I jump a little when, out of the corner of my eye, I see her right hand approaching my face. It's moving too slowly for a slap, so I calm down a bit as she puts her forefinger and thumb on either side of my chin, raises my face, and makes me look at her.

Her light brown almond-shaped eyes are a mirror of mine. We've both got the same eyes, the same light brown skin, the same dark brown hair and roughly the same skinny shape. Right now, my mom is about three inches taller than me. But if it weren't for her pudgy stomach and her wider hips (which she, of course, blames on me), we could probably trade jeans. Everybody says we look more like sisters than mother and daughter. She thinks it's a compliment. I don't. Who wants to look like her mother? But these eyes, they are both mine and hers. And just when I see a pool of tears forming in them, she points me toward the hallway and says, "I can't stand to look at you right now."

I wish she'd make up her mind. Does she want me to look at her or not?

Minutes later, we start with the all-too-familiar routine.

She comes into my room to collect my cell phone and my modem. I can keep the computer for the sake of school. I can go on the internet in the den, but only for academic purposes. There goes my social life.

"Where's the iPod?" she asks.

This is a new one. "That, too?" I protest. "Daddy gave it to me!"

She raises her eyebrows. "And?"

I cannot believe my mother is this mean! This is straight boo-dee, but I can't say so without getting into more trouble—not that that's possible at this point. Slowly, I reach into my Louis Vuitton drawstring bag and pull out the hot pink iPod, a gift my father gave me only two weeks ago to celebrate my sixteenth birthday. Unlike the other items she's taking away, this one hurts. I try real hard, but I can't stop the tears from falling down my cheeks. It feels like she's taking my daddy away from me. Again.

That's all she ever does is take, take, take. She takes my freedom, she takes my friends, my family, everything! I think she wants to take my life because she didn't have hers. She missed the homecoming games because she couldn't find a babysitter, she missed her senior prom because I had pneumonia, and she didn't graduate with her class because she had to sit out a semester. Basically, she lost her teen years when she got pregnant with me at sixteen—but how is that *my* problem? Why do I have to pay for her mistakes? I'm not my mom, and she's not me! The more I think about it, the madder I get.

My mother takes the iPod in hand and wraps the headphone cord around the rectangular box as she walks toward my bedroom door. I want to scream something from one of those poor little rich girl movies—something like "I wish I was never born!"—but there is always the possibility that my mother will do her best to make my wish come true by killing me now. The safest thing I *think* I can get away with while she's still in the room is crossing my arms on my chest. I'm pushing it.

Somehow, my mother sees me and says under her breath, "Keep on and you won't be getting a car for Christmas."

I know she did not just threaten me with the car my daddy has already promised me for Christmas when I pass my driver's test! "What's the point? It'll just be one more thing for you to take away from me." *Who said that?* I hold my breath and wait to see what my momma will bop me with. She's got a cell phone, a modem, and an iPod in hand. Those shouldn't hurt too badly.

She keeps her back to me as she grabs hold of the doorknob. She stops and takes a deep breath. I feel like I'm in a movie theater, waiting for the bad guy to jump out of the closet and attack the innocent victim. But instead, my mother says in a calm, even tone, "For your sake and mine, I'm gonna pretend I didn't hear that because I don't believe that God has called me into the prison ministry."

When my mother shuts the door behind her, I bury my face in my pillow and scream as loud as I can without letting her hear me. That's when the door opens again and my journal comes flying across the room, barely missing my head. I grab the journal and, for a moment, consider ripping each page to shreds. I still don't understand what gives her the right to read my stuff. In that whole forty-five-minute lecture she gave me, she never once mentioned the violation of my privacy. Where is the justice?

Instead of destroying my journal, I grab a pen from my desk and write:

Dear Me,

Mom just read my journal. Here is what I'm thinking:

#1— Nothing happened at Derrick's house, so I don't know what the big deal is.

#2— I can take care of myself, which was actually proven in the journal!

#3—What gives my mother the right to just go in my room and pick up my journal and read it?

#4— If my mom keeps me from getting the car that my daddy promised me, I will leave this house!

#5— Derrick does not look like Bow Wow. Do not ever fall for a guy that you have only seen from the 9th row up in the stands at a basketball game.

Maybe I should stop writing all of my personal stuff down. But if I do that, who will I tell all my problems? I mean, I have my friends, but they don't understand me like this journal does. No, I can't give up the journal. I will just have to find a good hiding place for it.

*   -Karis I've-Been-Wronged Reed*

Now I'm searching all over my room for a journal hideout spot. I've got to hide it in a place where it's so out of place no one would ever look there. There again, I have a problem. My mother might have the voice to be a minister, but she's got a nose that could outsniff a hound dog. She can smell trouble all over me. When I was little and I got a bad note from school, I could barely get off the bus before she'd say, "Something's wrong with you. What happened at school today?" And since

I've never been a good liar (at least not to my mother, anyway), I'd have to break down and tell her the truth, the whole truth, and nothing but the truth.

I'm searching through the closet now for a place big enough to hold a journal but small enough to be inconspicuous, and that's when I decide to forget it. Deep down inside, the truth is: I don't want to hide things from my mother. Once again, the tears start to sting my eyes. It bothers me that she read my journal. My mother and I have been living in this house alone for the last five years. When she and my father divorced, she got the house and me. She's always talking about how we only have each other and God. Always talking about how level-headed I am, what a blessing it is to have a daughter who is so self-reliant. So what made her think that she had to read my journal? What happened to the trust? In a way, I feel like she deserves whatever she got for reading it.

I figure the best thing I can do is stop writing in the journal until I'm eighteen, at which point I can do and write whatever because I will be *grown*. You hear me—*grown*! I cannot wait for that day! Go where I want to go, do what I want to do, answer to nobody but myself. And God, I suppose, but that shouldn't be too hard, since He already knows everything.

I close my journal and put it where I have always put it—in my top drawer. If I can't have my privacy and if my mother can't trust me, then . . . whatever. That's on her, except right now it's on me because I'm the one who's grounded. There's something seriously wrong with this picture.

chapter two

Later, just as I'm getting into the bathtub, I hear my mother knock on the bathroom door. "Yes?" I ask.

"I want to talk to you when you get out," she says from the other side.

"Yes, ma'am." I knew this was coming. The only thing worse than her yelling streak is the big huge talk after the yelling streak.

This will be the longest bath I have ever taken. I stay in the tub, staring at the hot pink accessories in my bathroom: curtain, rugs, toilet seat cover, toothbrush holder and soap dish. It's probably way too much hot pink for the average person, but not for me. Hot pink is my favorite color, and everyone who knows me knows it.

I guess I'm hoping my mother will just go to sleep and forget about talking to me. I figure this is as good a time as any to wash my hair. I undo the stopper in the tub and stand so that I can take a shower. Under normal circumstances, my mom would beat down the door and accuse me of making the water bill "sky high," but not tonight. She has other things on her mind, and so do I. I've got two more years to live in this house. How on earth am I going to live in peace knowing that at any minute my mom might raid my journal? My purse? My backpack? Who's to say she won't bust in on me right now?

I wish I could say all these things to my mom, but why waste my breath? She'll say, "I pay the bills around here. So long as I'm paying for the water you drink, the food you eat, and the electricity you use, there is nothing off limits for me in this house." Is that it? Do parents have a right to just do anything because they have jobs? I know she pays the bills and all, but there are some rights that I feel every human being should have, regardless of their employment status. I wonder if God would have gone through Jesus' things when he was a teenager. I know it's a moot point, but I just wonder.

Like I said, there's no need for me to tell these things to my mother. I can't win that argument no matter how much sense I make.

Twenty minutes later, I'm blow-drying my hair and my mother knocks on the door again.

"Karis, hurry up and come out of there. I've got to get up early tomorrow."

"Yes, ma'am."

I finish drying my hair. Lotion and powder come next, and I put on the Princess pajama set that my daddy gave me. I pull my long brown hair back into a ponytail and get ready for what is to come. I really don't know why my mother wants to have these long, boring conversations with me, where she tries to make me believe that she understands what I'm going through. *Pulleaze!* Her teenagehood—what she had of it— was way back in the last century. Things are different now; we have the internet, cell phones, harder classes, tougher laws, and much more responsibility than they had back in "the day" (as they call it). All of this means that while she might not have been ready to watch a movie with a guy when she was sixteen, that doesn't mean I'm not ready. I think I've listened to enough of her lectures and watched enough *Cosby Show* reruns to have a clue about boys.

Alas, I have finally reached the point where it's more painful to think about the big reflective talk than to endure it. I come out of the bathroom and drag my feet seven steps down the hallway to my bedroom, where my mother is waiting for me at the foot of my bed. She looks at me with arms folded and tired eyes. My eyes dart to the top drawer of my bureau, and I'm wondering if she has read my journal again.

She reads my mind and says, "You don't have to worry about me reading your diary again. For your information, I wasn't *trying* to read it this morning. You left it on your bed. Open. Did you know that? I thought maybe it was a home-work assignment that you'd forgotten. I looked at it to see if maybe I needed to bring it to you at school."

I'm thinking now; did I really leave it open? I guess . . . well, I had a few extra minutes, and I was just about to write in my journal this morning when Sydney called and told me that Avery McWilliams had asked her on a date, which is crazy, because everybody knows that Avery's on-again-off-again girlfriend, Iyanna Overton, will fight anybody who even sits next to Avery in class. Sydney was asking me if she should just forget about Iyanna and go out with Avery anyway. After all, it is a free world and Avery doesn't have any rings on his fingers. But I told Sydney to wait until after basketball season because if she ends up in a huge mess over Avery and gets suspended for fighting Iyanna, she might miss a game. That was serious business. Definitely serious enough to tear me away from the journal and forget that it was sitting on my bed as I left for school.

Okay, so maybe I left my journal out and it's not all my mom's fault. Doesn't matter. I can't admit that to her, because I cannot let her win this thing. She *still* didn't have to read it, and she *still* didn't have to take it to the extreme, and she *still* didn't have to take the iPod I got from my dad. I keep my attitude on display as my mother silently watches me lay my clothes out for tomorrow. Baby Phat jeans, a "Drama Queen" studded T-shirt, and white K-Swiss shoes.

My mother is still sitting there with her arms across her chest, waiting patiently for me to finish doing all the things I need to do before going to bed. I think she's enjoying this, because otherwise she would have told me to sit down a long time ago.

Finally I take out my contacts and put them in the case. My mother fusses, "You know you're supposed to wash your hands before handling your contacts. And haven't I told you to handle all of your contact lens business in the bathroom?"

If I take off my contacts in the bathroom I won't really be able to see what I'm doing when I lay out my clothes. Besides, my room is pretty clean. There can't be much danger from the bacteria in blue jeans and T-shirts. "I forgot," I lied for good reason.

"All right. You ain't gon' *forget* when you wake up blind

one morning," my mother exaggerates. Then she laughs at herself—or maybe at me. "Karis, Karis, Karis. It's so funny looking at you. You remind me so much of myself, with your rebellious streak. God forbid that you should make the same choices I made."

I am so sick of this line of reasoning! In frustration, I plop myself down next to my mom and plead as much as I can without sounding disrespectful. "Momma, I am *not* you! On your sixteenth birthday, you were pregnant. I was not. I'm already past that point, so you don't have to worry about me being *exactly* like you."

She lifts her hand to my head and pushes my bangs back behind my ears. My mother smiles at me now. "I'm proud of you, Karis. You have made it further than I did without getting pregnant. But, sweetheart, there's more to life than *not* getting pregnant. There's school, there's your future, and most importantly, there is your responsibility to fulfill your God-given purpose in life."

She's worried about stuff that is probably fifty years away. I don't see what any of this has to do with me here and now. "Momma, I'm not trying to be a minister like you. I just want to be . . . me."

"You can still be you and do what you're supposed to do. Actually, you can't fulfill your purpose *without* being the you that God created."

I swear, I am not trying to cause a distraction, but I notice a little wrinkle in the corner of her eye and I gasp, "Momma, don't move. There's something on your face."

She jumps up from the bed and makes a beeline to my mirror. She pulls at her face and asks, "What?"

I join her at the mirror and say, "Smile again."

She does, and I point out the tiny line that creaks into her face when she makes this gesture. She licks her finger and rubs spit into the line.

"Eww! That's nasty!" I shriek as I step away from her.

She chases me back to the bed and suddenly I'm laughing while my mother has wrestled me onto my right side, threatening to touch me with her spit-finger. I finally scream out, "Momma, you are too old for this!" She backs up off of me, catching her breath—which proves my point. She gives me a second to sit up, and when she tries to look at me, I look down at the floor. I haven't forgotten: I am still grounded and being unreasonably punished. That was sneaky of her to try to make me laugh.

When silence returns, she plays the love card. "You know I love you, right?"

My shoulders drop a little as I agree, "Yes, ma'am." She always gets to me with that one.

"And you know I'm not trying to make your life miserable. I'm only trying to be a good parent, right?"

"Yes, ma'am. I know. I just don't know why you have to be so hard on me."

My mother's eyebrows jump in amusement. "You think I'm hard?"

I nod in quick succession.

"You have no idea what hard is! Try being the only one who can't wear pants to PE class. Try making straight As or else getting grounded until the next report card! Try getting popped in the mouth for not saying 'yes, ma'am.' *That* is hard, Karis, and that's what I went through."

"Well, if Grandma and Grandpa were so hard on you, how did you end up pregnant with me at sixteen?" I'm asking this because I eventually want to work around to proving my theory that she should lighten up on me!

My mother looks down at her hands and shrugs. "My parents just gave me all the whats—what to do and what not to do. They never gave me the whys. I try my best to give you the rules and the reasons behind them, whenever possible. Not because I have to, but as a courtesy so that, hopefully, the lines of communication will stay open with us."

I shake my head. "I still don't understand why I can't do a lot of stuff."

My mom gives me a genuine smile. "I know you don't, Karis. You haven't lived long enough to see what I see and know what I know, so I can't expect you to reason as an adult would reason. But when you don't understand or trust my reasoning, just trust my heart, okay? Trust that I love you and that I'm trying to do what's best for you."

This conversation is deep—I'm trying to leave myself some wiggle room here. "Sometimes I'm not one hundred percent sure what you want me to do and what you don't want me to do. Sometimes, I think you think I can read your mind. Like that time I didn't know I was not allowed to eat in the bathroom."

"Don't even go there, Karis. This is different. You know good and well that it is not acceptable for you to be alone with a young man at his house," my mom says, putting a stop to all wiggle and jiggle room.

Well, she didn't *specifically* tell me I couldn't, but now is not the time to mention this tiny detail. "Yes, ma'am."

"And if you can't figure out whether it lines up with my standard, see if it's something you think God would approve of," my mother declares. "I think you've gone to enough

Sunday school, listened to enough sermons, and memorized enough verses in Awana to know right from wrong."

She's right. And I must admit to myself: the whole time I was at Derrick's house, there was this little voice within me saying that I should not be there.

My mother switches gears, taking me by surprise. "Now, you and Tamisha have been friends for a long time, and I don't appreciate her taking you over to that boy's house. I don't want to pick your friends for you, Karis, but if I have to—"

"It's not Tamisha's fault, Momma. I'm the one who asked her to take me over there. The whole thing was my idea." Lord knows, it was the truth. Lord also knows that I cannot afford to be banned from my only friend with a car—at least not until I get *my* car. Plus, if I don't stand up for Tamisha, there is a good chance that my mom will somehow get around to telling Tamisha's mom, and then we'd both be grounded forever.

"Well," my mother sighs, "don't let it happen again." She stands up, and when she does, I hear one of her knees make a popping sound. In addition to being a minister, my mother is a nurse. She stands on her feet all day, and I guess that makes your knees pop every once in a while. She turns toward me and holds out both hands. I know, immediately, that she wants to pray. I put my hands into hers and she seals them shut with a powerful grasp.

"Father," she prays, "we come to You now thanking You for Your protection; thanking You for watching over us even when we do foolish things. Thanking You for Your grace, and asking for more wisdom. Karis needs more wisdom in her role as a developing young lady, and, Lord, I need more wisdom as the mother of a developing young lady. We haven't been down this road before, but You have. You know all things. You said in Your word that if we would acknowledge You, You would direct our paths. So, we come before You asking for forgiveness and seeking Your guidance in all things. In Jesus' name we pray, amen."

"Amen," I repeat, wondering why my mom is asking for wisdom. From the way she talks, I thought she already knows everything (I mean that in a good way).

After the prayer is finished, she gives me a big hug and tells me to sleep tight.

As she walks away from me, I ask the burning question, "How long am I gonna be on punishment?"

"Until I say you're off." And she shuts the door behind her.

How crazy is that! I swear, sometimes I think parents are just making up the rules as they go.

chapter three

Dear Me:

I'm grounded—again! Partially because of this diary, partially because I did something I wasn't supposed to be doing, partially because my mom doesn't trust me. I'm not sure which is the biggest part.

I don't know if I spend more time grounded or ungrounded. It seems like every other week, I'm in trouble. Well, I gotta go to school now AND I gotta put this journal away!

Karis I-Just-Wanna-Be-Happy Reed

When I get to school, my girl Tamisha is waiting for me at my locker. I spot her long auburn weave all the way down the hallway and figure she'll be wearing red tones throughout the week. Tamisha is the only girl I know who tries to match her hair with her clothes. True to her game, she's wearing deep indigo jeans and a red DKNY short hooded sweater with the required undershirt barely covering her midriff. Tamisha is a little larger than most girls our age, but somebody forgot to tell her that. She wears the latest clothes, the cutest hairstyles, and she walks down the hallways like she owns them.

Today, Tamisha's shoes are bright red combination sneakers/heels that I tried to talk her out of, but Tamisha says I have so little fashion sense that my negative comment persuaded her to buy two pairs. When she sees me in the crowd, she walks toward me in a rush and follows me back to my locker. "Girl, I blew your cell phone up last night! Where were you? Why didn't you call me back?"

I look at her and roll my eyes. "I got in trouble, so I couldn't use my phone."

"What'd you get in trouble for?"

"That night you took me to Derrick's."

"That was, what, a month ago? How'd your mom find out?"

I sigh and admit, reluctantly, "My journal."

Tamisha slaps her own forehead, then looks at her hands to make sure she hasn't smeared her eyebrows. "Karis, you wrote about it in your journal? I've told you to quit putting all your dirt in writing! You're gonna get us both in trouble!"

I shake my head. "Don't worry. I told my mom that it was all my fault. You're clear."

She breathes in relief. "That was still stupid of you, Karis."

Sydney comes out of nowhere and completes the trio. "What was stupid?"

Tamisha turns toward our friend to fill her in on my tragedy. "This girl done wrote about her night with Derrick in her journal. Now her momma read it and she's in trouble."

"That *is* stupid," Sydney echoes.

I finish the combination and open my locker, wishing I could stuff myself inside. "Okay, already. I don't need a choir to sing it."

Sydney pulls a pen from her purse and puts on her best Britney Spears impression, singing to the tune of that *old* song we used to dance to in elementary school, "Oops, she did it again! She wrote it all down! Got caught in the game! Oh, baby, baby."

"Enough!" Tamisha stops Sydney by flashing two-inch nails in her face. "The White in you is *really* coming through today."

Sydney playfully pushes Tamisha's hand away. "Don't hate. I've got the best of two worlds." Sydney is biracial. Her mom is Black and her dad is White. When we were in middle school, people used to call Sydney "zebra"—up until the day Sydney gave Chelette Ingram a black eye for disrespecting her heritage. Sydney might have yellowish skin, green eyes, soft brown hair, and delicate features, but don't let the dimples fool you. Sydney ain't no punk. Plus, she's got mad basketball skills. Seriously. Everybody knows that Sydney Norman is going to a Division I college. She wants to be a lawyer like her father, but only after she's played a record ten years in the WNBA.

"Hey!" Sydney thinks a bit more about my situation and strikes the air with her fist. "This may go against the statute of limitations."

"The statue of who?" I ask.

Sydney practices her attorney skills on me. "The sta-*tute* of limitations. It's the rule that gives a time limit on how long a person has to bring charges against someone else in a court of law. How long ago was this Derrick incident—a month? Six weeks?"

I snarl up my face and smack my lips. "Please. My momma ain't got no statute of limitations. She'll go back to the day I was born if she wants to."

"Well," Sydney comes up with another argument, "how did she obtain the journal? Did she search through your things? Did she have a valid reason to be in your room? Because if she did not have a reasonable suspicion, the evidence is inadmissible and she cannot hold it against you."

That is so stupid I'm not even going to answer her. Sydney's got the kind of parents who try to talk things out with their kids, so I'm guessing that's why she's trying to build a case for me. But what Sydney does not understand is that my mother is unreasonable. She's not going to sit there and negotiate with me. My friends and I all know that my mom had no business reading my diary, but that is completely irrelevant in the court of Janice Reed. "All I know is I'm grounded indefinitely. So don't call me or text me; that'll only make things worse."

Sydney states for the record, "I, for one, think that you have been wrongfully grounded."

I roll my eyes at her as I continue to fish through my locker for all the books and folders that I will need for first period geometry and second period French II.

"Do you want to call Ms. Reed and let her know how you feel?" Tamisha questions Sydney. I'm glad that Tamisha is feeling me on this. Sometimes I think Sydney lives in a different world. It's nice to have someone who can kind of bridge the gap between Sydney and me.

Sydney considers Tamisha's proposal and decides not to say anything else. Sydney purses her lips, and the dimples in her cheeks rest her case. I close my locker and the three of us walk toward the intersection of two major hallways.

As we prepare to split up, Sydney offers her own form of justice. "You wanna use my little sister's cell phone? Really, Angelique never uses it. Half the time she doesn't know where it is, and the other half of the time, she doesn't have it charged up."

This is an excellent idea. Well, I mean it's not an *excellent* idea, but . . . well . . . when I really, really think about it, this whole grounding thing is kind of not my fault in the first place. If my mom wasn't so busy trying to punish me for the mistakes she made sixteen years ago, maybe I wouldn't be grounded to begin with. Now *that* is as good a reason as any to bend the rules a little bit. "Cool." I perk up now in response to Sydney. It's so good to have friends who understand me.

"Just remember—free time doesn't start until after six."

"What about weekends?" I ask.

"Free all day. I'll bring the phone and the charger tomorrow."

"Thanks, Sydney. I owe you one."

Next I turn to Tamisha. "How much time 'til the bell?" Tamisha's watch is set with the school's clock.

"One minute forty seconds, and we haven't even discussed *my* life yet. I am having a serious problem."

Tamisha is my girl and all, but her problems tend to be directly or indirectly related to fashion, and I am not about to get another tardy for some Apple Bottoms issue. Nelly is fine, but he ain't gonna be at my house when the report card arrives, and he sure won't be putting any money toward my college tuition. I have to keep my grades up so I can earn scholarships. Tamisha's fashion problem will have to wait. "I gotta go," I brush her off. "Write a note and put it in my locker or we can just wait 'til we get to fourth period, okay?" I offer as an apology while readjusting my backpack and taking a few steps away from her, toward my class.

Tamisha takes a deep breath, then says, "It can wait 'til fourth period."

"You okay?" Sydney's tone is sincere, and it stops me cold.

The one-minute warning bell rings and the hall suddenly begins to clear. I see Tamisha's bottom lip start to quiver, then she quickly tucks it between her teeth. This must be serious, because there is no way Tamisha would be blurring her lipstick for nothing. "Fourth period."

I should have just been tardy for first period, because all morning long, I keep thinking about Tamisha's stressed-out face. I take notes about these theorems and postulates in geometry class, but I really can't concentrate on what any of them mean.

After first period, I rush out to see if I can catch Tamisha before second period, but I'm too late. She is already off the B hall. After second period, I see Sydney between classes, and she's just as concerned as I am. Neither of us has a clue about what could be wrong with Tamisha. Sydney and I run down the list of possibilities as we both hang out in the hallway in the final minutes before the bell.

"Okay, I think her grades are fine," Sydney says. "Otherwise, she wouldn't still have the keys to her car."

I cross the biggest thing off the list. "Well, we know it's not a boy problem, 'cause there's no one on her radar right now. Oh, wait!" I remember. It's a long shot, but there was this guy that Tamisha liked a few weeks ago. "What about what's-his-name? Robert? The one from California?"

"No way." Sydney shakes her head. "He has rough lips and she almost threw up when they kissed. Robert is definitely out of the picture. Think of something else."

"Maybe her parents are getting divorced," I suggest.

Sydney's imagination is far worse. "Maybe she's sick with leukemia or something."

Now I'm getting really depressed, and I can see that Sydney is starting to feel it, too. I've known Tamisha since the first day of fourth grade. If something happens to her, I know my life will never be the same. I can't take all this sadness anymore, so I lighten the mood with a joke. "Maybe Dooney & Bourke is going out of business."

Sydney looks down at me, rolls her eyes, then busts out laughing. "You know you're crazy, right?" She smiles again and I feel better, hoping that no matter what is wrong with Tamisha, we'll be able to laugh about it by the end of our English class.

chapter four

Third period drags on forever, because Mr. Allen shows the most boring, stupid DVD ever created. I don't even know why people are still making movies about 1720; it's over. The world is *way* past the eighteenth century now, which is exactly what I write in the editorial paragraph that he assigns following the movie. I'm not worried about it, though, because Mr. Allen won't even read it. He'll just put a big red check mark on it for a participation grade. As much as I can't stand Mr. Allen's social studies class and as completely pointless as it can be, there are definite advantages to having a coach for a teacher. They *never* read the essays.

Finally, fourth period arrives. Sydney and I take our seats in the back right corner of the room. Mrs. Clawson is cool— she lets us do what we want so long as we get our work done. When we're preparing to read a novel, we have about a week of busywork (vocabulary and historical background stuff). She gives us the busywork packet on Monday, and we work at our own pace. Sometimes she lets us work in groups—it just depends on how much the other classes have gotten on her nerves.

Tamisha walks in and sits at the table with Sydney and me. We've still got a few minutes until the bell. "Okay, so what's so important?" I ask.

"Yeah," Sydney presses. "What's up?"

Suddenly, that same somber look crosses Tamisha's deep brown face as she barely whispers, "My brother has to go to Iraq."

My heart sinks down in my chest. *Marlon, in Iraq?* "How can they make him go to Iraq? He just graduated from high school! He's only eighteen!" I say in disbelief.

"That's gotta be against the law," Sydney protests as she slams an open hand on her English book.

Tamisha makes a square on her desk with her arms and buries her face within that square, sobbing uncontrollably. I crawl onto the floor and put an arm around Tamisha while Sydney does the same on the other side. I can't stand to see Tamisha like this, all sad and crying. Then Sydney starts crying, too, and I can't stop the tears from flowing down my face. Next thing you know, we're all crying and there's a little huddle forming around us while Mrs. Clawson directs the last few students into the classroom.

I feel someone touch me on the back and I rise up slightly. It's Margarita Hernandez. She hands me a tissue. If anyone has a tissue, it's Margarita. I see her crying all the time over some boy or another. She asks, "What's wrong?" I look behind her and see two other faces staring down at us. I'm not really sure if I should tell her, because everyone who knows anybody at Central High School knows Marlon Banks. I'm not sure if Tamisha is ready for the onslaught of Mrs. Marlon Banks wannabees who will surely mob her after school for Marlon's mailing address when word gets around school that Marlon is in Iraq. I imagine it's hard being smart, athletic, funny, popular, and attractive at the same time. Marlon managed to do all of those things well.

Tamisha looks up for a moment and whispers, "My brother is going to Iraq."

Margarita does the sign of the cross and says something in Spanish. Then she says, "I'm so sorry, Tamisha. My uncle is over there already. He says it's not so bad. He sends me pictures in email all the time. Your brother will be fine."

Tamisha wipes her face and tries to pull herself together. "Thank you, Margarita."

When I see that Tamisha is going to be okay, I get back into my desk and scoot myself a little closer to her. Mrs. Clawson comes into the room and tells us to take out our packets and get to work. Tamisha, Sydney, and I pull out the papers, but it's no use. We can't work. No one in the room can work, actually, because they are all so busy writing little notes to Tamisha, telling her how their brothers or cousins or aunts are serving in Iraq. By the end of the class period, someone has initiated a list. Everyone who has a friend or loved one serving in the military signs his name and the soldier's name on the list. Tamisha doesn't really know what to do with it, so somehow I end up with that list in my possession.

When I get home after school, I keep looking at the list. So many names, so many people. And there is Marlon's name—Marlon Banks. Marlon Banks. A few years ago, I used to say that name in my dreams. I had the biggest, hugest crush on him. It was kind of funny. After all those years of kicking him out of Tamisha's room and plotting with Tamisha to kill his beloved pet lizard, all of a sudden he got cute when we were in eighth grade and he was in tenth. I tried to hint around to Tamisha that I kinda thought her brother was cute, but all she said was "Euuu! That is too nasty—my brother and my best friend?" Her reaction was so visceral that I knew I had to let it go. Besides, Marlon always had a lot of females chasing him, and I knew I didn't have a chance against those older girls.

And now he's about to go to war. Maybe even die.

I fold up the list and take a few steps toward the trash, but I can't throw the names away. That wouldn't be right. This list is too important; all these people in harm's way, with families and friends worrying about them all the time. How could I throw their names away without doing something? I sit down on my bed and let my eyes roll across their names again.

I still can't believe it. Marlon is going to Iraq.

I'm wondering what I am going to do with this list when suddenly it hits me: I can pray. I'm actually surprised by this thought, because it sounds like something my mom would say. She's always praying for people. Praying like there's no to-morrow. Well, there might not be a tomorrow for Marlon and the rest of those on the list, so I guess praying is all I *can* do for them. It's not like I can call up the Prez and tell him to call the whole thing off. I can't even vote yet—probably because I don't pay taxes yet. Hmph, another one of those grown-up-made systems that only benefits them. I'm glad God doesn't have an age or wage minimum on who can contact Him. I would be totally stuck out!

My mom has several books on prayer, I remember. I've seen them in her room lots of times when I'm dusting. I don't usually go into her room when she's not here, but this is an emergency. People are dying and I've got to do something. I ease into her room and take a few steps toward her bookshelf. My momma's got enough books for a whole year's worth of reading; books on nursing, books about God, books about being a woman, novels. My mom is a total bookworm.

Her mauve comforter is neatly pressed across her bed, and the shammed pillows are set in place perfectly. Her nightstand, just beside her bed, shows the only sign of disarray. She's got two books opened flat, a glass of water, and her Bible sitting at the base of the lamp.

It seems like the bookshelf takes up more room than the bed does, but I know exactly where to look for the books on prayer. I pick one that reads *Praying for Your Loved Ones* on the spine. I flip to the index and find Prayers for Protection. I just skim through the section and find the shortest prayer, which reads:

Heavenly Father,
Send your angels of protection to guard _____
during this time of testing in his/her life. Let _____
come to know You as the Good Shepherd who watches over His
flock with diligence and love. Amen.

I grab a sticky note and a pen from my mother's dresser and jot down the prayer. Then I flip back to the index to see if there's any other chapter that might have better—or shorter—prayers. As I'm flipping through the pages, something catches my eye. That something is my name. Karis here, Karis there,

Karis everywhere! My momma is praying for just about everything for me! She must think I'm doing all kinds of crazy stuff!

I slam the book shut and put it back on the shelf. I don't know if I should be grateful that she thinks so much of me, or offended that she's praying for me like I'm some kind of heathen. I wish she would just relax and know that I can take care of myself.

When I get back to my room, I power up my computer and type the prayer in really pretty font so I can put it in my journal. While I'm at it, I decide to copy and paste so that Tamisha can have one. Sydney, too. And maybe one for Margarita as well. We've gotta pray this prayer, because I don't know about those other people, but Marlon is way too much fineness to be wasted in a war.

chapter five

True to her word, Sydney brings the cell phone and charger to school the next day. When I take the phone from her, I have to take a deep breath and push out all the second thoughts I'm having about using this phone while I'm grounded. I remind myself: I have been wrongfully punished, therefore I have every right to use this phone. Besides, there is no way I can live without some kind of connection to the world outside my prison-house.

Tamisha's number is the first to be programmed into Angelique's phone. I relax now, reveling in the idea of having a life again. I'll have to remember to turn off the ringer in the afternoons so my mom won't catch me, but at least I can return calls after six o'clock.

I give Tamisha and Sydney the prayer that I printed out for Marlon, and they look at me a little weird. "What?" I ask as we walk toward the gym for the JV pep rally. No one really comes to the JV football games, but if we happen to be at school too early on a cold Thursday morning, the pep rally is a warm spot to meet with friends.

"Following in your mom's footsteps, huh?" Sydney smirks.

"No." I roll my eyes at her. I go to church and all, but the last thing I want people to think is that I'm like my mother. It's bad enough I look like my mom. Don't get me wrong; my mom is cute. But when I look in the mirror and see her light brown eyes looking back at me, it's like she's fussing at me to take off some of my lipgloss and stand up straight.

Sydney has different ideas about religion. Her family believes in God, but they don't go to church. The first time she told me that, we were in third grade, and I was in shock. I couldn't imagine *not* going to church on Sunday. I didn't even know the option existed. "What do you *do* on Sunday mornings?" I asked her.

"Sleep," was her reply as she looked at me like *"Duh."*

Now, as she questions my religiousness, I feel the need to defend myself. "You don't have to be a minister to pray."

Sydney shrugs, folds up the prayer, and stuffs it into her back pocket.

Tamisha, on the other hand, is eager to hear my thoughts on the prayer. Her family has a church home, but they don't go every Sunday because sometimes her parents work on the weekends. And now that Tamisha has a job at JC Penney, she goes even less. "How often do you think we should say this prayer?"

"I don't know. I guess once a day."

"Cool. Once a day," Tamisha agrees with me as she glances down at the words once more before sliding the prayer into the clear front pocket of her three-ring binder. It has suddenly become more important than all the pictures and drawings beneath.

We enter the gym, and we are instantly the center of attention. I hate the moment when everyone is staring at you as you walk through the doors. We're in Sydney's territory, so she leads the way to the cool section of the stands and our circle suddenly grows larger as we say hello to our substitute friends—the ones Tamisha, Sydney, and I talk to when we can't find each other. All at once, we just blend in with the pretty girls, the kick-your-butt-and-ask-questions-later girls, the boys who used to blow spitballs at us, some of whom are now so fine that I can't believe how much we used to hate them in elementary school. We're a group now. The class of 2009-2012. A few rows up, Ronald Hartsfield and J. J. Thompson are telling old "your momma" jokes, and everyone is laughing because the jokes are so corny. We're all totally ignoring the vice principal as she talks about something or another that no one cares about.

Iyanna Overton taps Tamisha on the shoulder, and we both look up at her. "I'm sorry about Marlon. I hope he's gonna be okay."

Tamisha gives her a half-grin and blinks back the tears. "Thanks."

I look over at Sydney, who just heard what I heard, and I know she's thinking the same thing I'm thinking: maybe she shouldn't steal Iyanna's man after all.

My father arrives at 5:30 on the dot to pick me up for our great and glorious weekend together. My suitcase is in the back and I'm sitting in the front seat of his black Mitsubishi

Montero, watching him talk to my mother at the front door. I know what they're saying. She's telling him that I'm grounded and that I can't do this or that. He's asking why I'm grounded and telling her that he will do his best to make sure I stay grounded, but I know my daddy. There's no such thing as "grounded" when I'm with him. Even if he did try to ground me, being with him is as good as being ungrounded, so it doesn't matter.

If I had any kind of nerve, I would reach over and blow the horn so he'd hurry up and come on, but I know my momma would beat me down for that. Instead, I start snooping around my dad's car, careful to keep one eye on him. I slowly open the glove compartment. Breath mints. Business cards. Nothing to write home about. Next, I explore the compartment in the middle console. Nothing there except a phone charger and a few stale CDs.

He is still talking to my mother and, by the looks of their body language, this is not going well. I try real hard to pick up on what they're saying, but with the hum of the engine, I can only pick up on a few phrases: "bad example," "Christian home." Well, whatever they're arguing about, I'm sure it's stupid. They used to argue over every little thing right before they divorced. I remember one time they had an argument because my dad wouldn't turn on the heat in the car. I wanted to reach up and turn it on myself, I was so sick of them fighting. Today is just like old times.

My dad eventually gets into the car and slams the door behind him. Before I try talking, I wait until we are on the Interstate and he has listened to a few songs. I can tell by the way his thick lips flatten out and the line in his forehead disappears that he is finally okay.

"So, what are we going to do this weekend?" I start the conversation.

He shrugs uneasily. "Not much."

Cool. I don't mind just hanging out—watching TV, ordering pizza, and stuff. Actually, that's what I like to do with my dad. Sometimes he pulls out old 1980s movies and I laugh like crazy at the silly haircuts and the break dancing. I don't really like the movies, but my dad seems to enjoy remembering what he calls "the good ole days."

"You got some old movies?" I ask.

"Well," he hesitates, "I was thinking we might do a little something."

I perk up in my seat. "Like what? You wanna go do something crazy like laser tag? Or how about ice-skating at the Galleria?"

"No. I was wondering . . . do you mind if we . . . have a little company?"

"Who?" I ask.

My dad blurts out, "Her name is Shereese. She's my girl-friend."

I feel like stopping the car and getting out right here on the freeway. Is he crazy? I could hardly sleep last night for thinking about spending time with my daddy, and now he wants to bring some chick into the picture? I don't think so. "No," I say, looking out the window and away from him.

"I really think you'll like Shereese. She's looking forward to meeting you." His attempt at smoothing things over is not working. He should have told me all of this before I hopped my happy behind into his car. I don't feel like sharing my dad with someone else, no matter how much she wants to meet me.

"She's a nice person. Here. Here's a picture," he says as he flips down his visor. *He keeps a picture of her in his visor? What kind of corny mess is that?* I take a look at her. She has a short, spiky haircut—the kind that you just wrap up at night, scrunch up in the morning, throw on a little spritz, and go. It matches her thin, light-brown face perfectly. Her lips are to die for—perfect heart shape. She's not wearing a lot of makeup. Her eyebrows are perfectly arched, high cheekbones, flawless skin. Her hand is just beneath her chin, so I see she's got the same nails my mom wears.

She's very pretty. Actually, she's a little too pretty for my daddy, if you ask me. I could see her getting real boo-ji on me. She's also rather young, I'm thinking. "How old is she?"

My dad waits a second, like he has to think about it. He might say that it's none of my business, but he might as well tell me because if he doesn't tell me, I'll ask her myself. "She's twenty-four."

"Twenty-four! That's only eight years older than me!"

"I'm only thirty-two." My dad tries to play it off like it's nothing. I betcha he would not even hear me if I told him I had a boyfriend who was eight years older than me! "Shereese and I have been dating for several months and I think it's time that the two of you got to know each other."

"Oooh." I shake my head and give him back the picture. I can't believe this. I get to spend one weekend a month with my dad and now I have to spend it with some girl who's probably nothing but a gold digger. Well, my daddy doesn't have any gold, but why can't she find somebody her own age, and why can't he just be happy being single, like my mom?

chapter six

Thirty minutes later, when we pull into his driveway, I realize that he's not really asking me if I want to meet Shereese. He has already arranged for us to meet, because there's another car, a Honda Accord with sorority license plates on it, in the driveway. "She's already here?" I protest to my father.

"She lives here," he informs me.

"You got a woman living with you!" I yell. Now I know what he and my mother were arguing about. I'm ready to go back home.

My dad looks over at me, his eyes pleading. His bushy eyebrows are raised high, and he asks politely, "I don't ask much of you, Karis, because I know the divorce was hard on you. But can you give Shereese a chance, okay? Just do this one thing for your daddy, all right?" He reaches over and tilts my face toward his.

I don't answer him with words; I just get out of the car and stand there beside my door as he gets my bags from the back and escorts me to the front door of his house. His house is smaller than the house that my mom and I live in. He's got three bedrooms, but he only has one bathroom, a living room, and one dining area. He has a big backyard with a covered patio. I told him he should get a pool, but so far he hasn't listened to my suggestion.

Shereese greets us at the door, and she is just as pretty as her picture, if not prettier. Her skin is model-smooth, and I know she's had that whitening thing done on her teeth. Honestly, I couldn't have found a prettier girl for my dad if I'd tried— which I certainly would not! She's wearing frayed jeans, layered shirts, and no shoes. No shoes! Why is she walking around my father's house barefoot?

"Hi, Karis." She holds out her hand and I shake it. "I've heard so much about you."

"Hello, Shereese." *I haven't heard jack about you.*

Now, as I step into the living room, I see that my dad has made a few changes. The love seat and sofa have been switched, which actually makes the room look bigger. He's got an area rug under the coffee table, and there's an abstract painting above the chaise. Shereese is taking over!

With my father bringing up the rear, Shereese leads me toward my room—like I really need her to show me the way to my own bedroom at my father's house. When she opens the door, I have the hugest surprise right before my eyes. My room has been totally redecorated with hot pink and black everything! It's beautiful! I have a hot pink shag rug, a canopy with hot pink fuzzy things all around the edges. My bedspread is white, with a hot-pink-and-black '50s-style poodle, and the shams have the cutest little stuffed poodle sitting between them. There's a huge hot pink lava lamp that's as tall as me in the corner, and there are hot pink frames with some of my favorite singers—Bow Wow, Destiny's Child, and Kirk Franklin. I could live and die in this room!

"Do you like it?" my father asks.

I can't help myself. "I love it!"

"Shereese decorated it for you. I told her your favorite color, and she took it from there," my father explains.

I could give Shereese a big bear hug right now, but I won't. Even though she obviously went through a lot to get this room ready for me, a genuine smile will have to do. "Thank you, Shereese. It's beautiful."

I can tell that she's a little disappointed that I'm not turning cartwheels right now, because her eyes kind of go down a little and that smile on her face collapses into a straight line. "You're welcome."

"We'll let you get settled in," my dad says as he pulls Shereese out by the hand. Okay, maybe I was wrong for not expressing my joy. The fact is, though, my dad is wrong for throwing this girl in my face—even if she does have mad decorating skills.

Really, I don't want to unpack my things. I feel like calling my mother and telling her what's going on. Wait, she already knows what's going on. She must think that I can handle this. I take a look at myself in the mirror and have a little self-talk: *I can handle this. I am mature. I am sixteen.*

I need help. I pull out Angelique's phone and call Tamisha

to tell her what's going on in my once stable world now turned upside down.

"Your dad is definitely robbing the cradle," Tamisha agrees. "And if she's as pretty as you say she is, why can't she find somebody her own age?"

"I know!"

We call Sydney on three-way. Sydney has always thought my dad is pretty cute, so she understands how he hooked up with someone who is young enough to be my big sister from another mother.

"I'll call you guys later tonight and tell you how it goes," I tell them both.

"I'm working late—we've got inventory," Tamisha says.

Sydney adds, "I'm going to bed early. We've got a tournament tomorrow morning."

I let out a frustrated sigh. "So what am I supposed to do when I get back? Talk to a wall?"

"Get over yourself, Karis," Sydney advises. "Sounds like Shereese is pretty cool to me."

Turns out that Sydney is right. Friday night, my dad, Shereese, and I go to the movies and out to eat. At the movie theater, Shereese talks him into letting me see an R-rated movie—my mom would kill him if she found out about it! Actually, that was the movie I saw on bootleg DVD at Derrick's house, but I really don't want to go into all that with my dad. The less he knows the better. The only thing that is kind of weird about the movie is that my dad sits between Shereese and me. When the scary part comes, we are both trying to hold on to him and he is sitting here trying to figure out which one of us to lean his head toward. I try to remember how things were when my mom, my dad, and I used to watch movies when I was little, but it just won't come to me.

After the movie, we go to Joe's Crab Shack and throw down on some crab legs. My dad is trying to be all proper, but me and Shereese are sloppin' up that food and throwing the shells in the bucket like nobody's business. I'm so full I have to unbutton the top button on my pants and let it all hang out. Shereese does, too.

All the way home we listen to the new 105.7 radio station. They're playing a few songs that my dad likes, but mostly they play stuff that Shereese and I sing to, loud and off key. My dad turns the radio down a few times and Shereese keeps turning it back up. She and I laugh like crazy and I'm starting to feel that maybe my dad is more like my mom than I ever realized. He's acting like he's . . . all old and tired.

When we get home, it's late and we're all tired. I go to my room and they go to theirs—my dad's room—and suddenly this whole picture doesn't seem right. Shereese is cool: it's this whole setup that I don't like. My dad is in his bedroom with some young chick while my mom is probably sitting at home all alone, reading a book. Okay, here comes the truth: I've always hoped that some day my mom and dad would get back together. There, I've said it. It's not something I think about all the time. In fact, I stopped asking God for that a long time ago. It's just one of those things where you think, "Wouldn't it be nice if that happened?" but you don't hold your breath and you don't think any more about it because nothing seems to be happening with it one way or another. And, so long as nothing was happening to kill the dream, I could always keep the secret hope-flame alive. Until now.

This is getting pretty depressing, so I decide to call my

favorite lab partner, Jordan Taylor. Somehow, we always end up in science classes together. He likes me, but I don't like him for anything more than a friend. I think he has a girlfriend now, so I have to be careful. Girls these days can be pretty crazy. I fish Angelique's phone from my purse and try my best to remember Jordan's phone number. The first number I call is somebody who speaks Spanish. The second number is some old man who cusses me out for calling so late with the wrong number. "I'm sorry," I apologize as I make a mental note to myself: *get phone numbers from other phone.*

The third time, I get a guy who sounds a little like Jordan, but I'm not sure. "May I speak to Jordan?"

"This is Jordan."

"Jordan Taylor?"

"I'm Jordan-whoever-you-want-me-to-be," the stranger flirts.

How lame. "I'm sorry. I think I've got the wrong number."

"Wait, wait. Don't hang up. What's your name?"

"I don't talk to strangers." Click.

This Jordan wannabee calls me back in five seconds flat. "I love you."

"You are sick. Don't call me anymore," I give him in my best don't-mess-with-me tone.

"I'm gonna call you every day and make you fall in love with me. What's your name?"

"If you call me every day, I'm gonna pray for you every day," I threaten further. "Starting right now. Father in Heaven, I pray for this wacko on the phone—"

Click. He hangs up this time and I give up on getting in touch with Jordan tonight. Obviously, it wasn't meant to be.

The only other guy whose phone number I do know by heart is Quinten Wilson. He and I had history class together last year. He's cool and I really don't know why we never got past a friendship, but it's okay. He's not the kind of guy who's immediately attractive. You have to kind of talk to him, and then he starts doing nice things for you like bringing Cheetos to class for you and letting you *have* (not borrow) a pen so you can do your work. And you start thinking to yourself, "He's not all that cute, but I could make an exception." Then one day you see him talking to another girl in the hallway and it hits you: you like him. I started liking Quinten around Christmastime last year, but he had a girlfriend by then. They broke up after Valentine's Day, but I had a boyfriend by then. That's just how it has always been between me and Quinten; friends until fate says otherwise.

I remember his number because it's 214-555-LOVE. We discovered this on the day that he gave me his number and I programmed it into my cell phone. He told me that from then on, whenever he gave a girl his number, he always won extra points for the "LOVE."

I call his number and he answers, "Whodis?"

"Who you *think* dis is?"

"Stop playin'. Who is this?"

I smack my lips. "Oh, I guess you *got* it like that. So many girls calling, you can't tell one from the other?"

"This must be Karis, the heartbreaker."

I have to admit, it feels good that he recognizes my voice. "Whatever! Sounds to me like you're the one breaking hearts."

He laughs softly. "Whatchu doin', callin' a brother all late at night?"

"Nothin'. Over my dad's house for the weekend. What are you up to?"

"Say, I'm out with my girl right now. You got about two minutes until she comes back from the restroom. Whassup?"

"So, who's the lucky lady these days?" I ask.

"Could be *you* if you'd give a brother a chance."

"Whatever, Quinten." I smile. "You're the one with J. Lo syndrome: can't wait five minutes before you're with somebody else."

He laughs, and I can see his beautiful, bright teeth in my mind's eye. "Oh, that hurt. That hurt. I gotta go, though. You gonna be up later tonight?"

"Yeah. Call me on this number."

"Straight. Bye."

"Bye."

I don't really expect Quinten to call, and he doesn't. That's how it is with guys sometimes. When you talk to them, they're all yours. But when you hang up, it's like whatever.

Well, my dad is in his room with his girlfriend. My mom is at work, my friends are out of reach, and I don't have any guy friends to talk to. Looks like it's just me and my journal tonight.

Dear Me:

What a boring night! Well, it wasn't all boring. I had a good time with my dad and his GIRLFRIEND. She seems all right. I'm just not used to seeing my dad all hugged up with anyone. He did look kinda happy, though. I wish my mom could be happy in love again, but she's so busy working and speaking and taking care of me because she thinks I'm a wild child. I'm really not wild—I am just independent. I have my own mind.

You know what I really wish? I really wish I had a boyfriend. Someone to talk to, someone who cared about me and could really give me a boy's perspective on things. I could help him with his problems and he could help me with mine. My friends are okay, but you can't really flirt with your friends. Plus, I just like the way boys' voices sound—they're not all squeaky like ours. They're deep and calm and . . . I don't know. I'm not boy crazy, but it's nice how different they are from us. Now if we could just get all the cute ones to stop being dogs! Ha! Okay, I know that's not nice. Sorry, God, if you're reading this. I know You made boys, too.

Ciao!

Karis Looking-for-Mister-Right Reed

I put my journal away and say the prayer for Marlon before crawling between the new sheets and comforter. As I drift off to sleep, my mind roams to my mom. Back when I was little and my parents were broke young newlyweds, I often had to go to work with her and hang out in the waiting room until my dad got off work and could pick me up. I loved being at the hospital with her because no matter how late it was, they didn't turn off the lights. I was simply amazed and overjoyed that it was never dark in the hospital.

Now I imagine my mother standing at the nurse's station, reading charts and working through the night. I know that she loves helping people, but sometimes I wish she didn't have to work so much. If she could get back with my dad, they could maybe split the bills, and then she could dedicate more time to speaking and ministering. And being with me.

chapter seven

The good thing about being middle class is that your parents don't have money to throw away. Since my mom already paid the deposit on my driver's education course and already arranged to be off work in the evenings for three weeks in a row so she could take me back and forth to classes, driver's education became an investment that she couldn't take back. So, here I am back at my mom's house. Still grounded, but still on track for my car just the same. *Yes!*

The first night, my mom lets me know that she is not exactly excited about taking me to class. "After this situation with the young man, you don't deserve this, you know?" she fusses.

"I know," I agree for the sake of peace. She parks directly in front of the building and unlocks the door.

I swing the door open, ready to embrace this new level of freedom in my life. As soon as I start driving, my life is going to be *so* on. I get one foot out of the car and my mom changes her tune from fussy to concerned. "Be careful, Karis, and pay attention. Driving is a serious responsibility."

I look back at my mom to assure her that I am not a baby anymore. I am perfectly capable of driving, being a young lady in the company of boys, and probably a million other things that she thinks I can't do. "I'll be careful, Mom." I close the car door and she drives off as I'm walking into the building. *Finally!*

Our driver's education classroom looks like any other classroom—rows of seats and chairs—except we're in an office suite. I recognize some of the kids from my school. I'd say about half of them are from Central; the other half are probably from either Carter, Cedar Hill, or Duncanville. I'm looking around my room to see if my future perfect boyfriend could possibly be in this class. It's a bust. No cute guys, no fine guys. It's just a room full of people that I could see in any given class at Central High School.

Everyone says they try to scare us the first day with all these films of dead people so we'll take driving seriously. Really, the way the laws are here in Texas, they have taken all the fun out of driving. No more than two teens in a car after a certain time, no driving after certain hours in some cities unless you have an adult in the car. It's crazy, like they really don't want us driving in the first place.

We sit in class for three whole nights watching gory films and reviewing the handbook. This is so boring! I mean, really, I've been riding in cars since the day I came home from the hospital. I know what a stop sign is!

I am so ready to get behind the wheel. I just hope I don't have to go driving with this teacher named Mr. Chauncey. He is seriously scary. For one thing, he has a patch over his left eye. I don't know who approved him to teach teens how to drive when he can hardly see what we're doing. He also has some scars on his hands. People have been whispering that the reason they keep him around is because he *can't* die. They say he's been in all kinds of wrecks with the students but he always survives, so they can't fire him.

My first time behind the wheel, I go with a girl named Jerricka. Our instructor is a young lady named Rebecca, who insists that we call her Miss Rebecca. She is probably around Shereese's age, only she dresses like she's thirty-five. She's wearing cotton pants and a fleece sweater with a big kitten on the front. My fashion prayer is that I never wear such clothes before I turn forty. No, fifty.

Jerricka drives for the first hour and I sit in the backseat listening to Miss Rebecca fuss the whole time. I could have done better with my momma. "Slow down! Speed up! Yield—you don't have the right of way!" Every once in a while, Jerricka looks over her shoulder and rolls her eyes toward Miss Rebecca. I feel her—this woman is in the wrong profession. "Keep your eyes on the road, Jerricka!"

Then, it's my turn. I slap hands with Jerricka and we trade. Now she's in the back and I'm in the driver's seat. We start off in a parking lot just looking at the gears and adjusting the mirrors. Miss Rebecca tells me that I should have about an inch of the car in my sideview mirror. "An inch?" I ask. She's confusing me, so I just say "yeah" when she asks if the mirrors are okay. How am I supposed to know if they're okay? *She's* the teacher. Finally, after about thirty minutes of just going around in circles, we head out to a real street with stop signs and lanes and real people walking along the sidewalk. My heart is racing and my hands get all sweaty. I've seen people driving all my life, but now that I'm behind the wheel, it's different. My life is literally in my hands, and I don't know if I'm ready for all this.

"Take a few deep breaths, Karis. You'll be okay," Miss Rebecca says to me. Now I wish she was thirty-five because at least it wouldn't seem like the blind leading the blind.

Jerricka gives a shot of confidence. "You got this, girl."

I take that deep breath and put my foot on the accelerator. We jerk out of the parking lot so fast my head hits the headrest. In seconds, I'm screeching onto the street. Rebecca's clenching the door handle and slamming her foot on the special brake installed for instructors. Jerricka screams out a few choice cuss words. "Let me outta here! This girl can't drive!"

Miss Rebecca yells back to her, "Jerricka, we are all learning—"

"Whatever! She ain't gotta learn with *my* life! I ain't ridin' with her!"

What happened to the camaraderie? The sisterhood?

"Okay," our instructor squeaks as she rubs her neck. It takes her a moment to come back to herself, and then she instructs me to reverse this car right back into the parking lot so we can work on the basics again. This is the worst night of my existence. Jerricka goes back and tells everybody what a loser-driver I am. Kids are snickering at me when I walk back into the building.

By the time I get ready to drive on Thursday, people are all pairing up with their newfound friends. Not even Miss

Rebecca wants to drive with me. Now I have to drive with Mr. Chauncey and some boy who looks like he's twelve years old. I don't even think he can see over the steering wheel. I guess they figure if anyone can survive this boy and Karis Reed driving, it's the immortal Mr. Chauncey.

The boy, whose name is Elgin, drives first. I want to give him a hairclip because he keeps slinging his bangs back every five seconds. He's got chains hanging all down his legs, pants so long they make a sleeve around his tennis shoes. This boy looks crazy, like he might decide at any moment to kill us all. I'm just making sure my seat belt is on right.

This hour is killing me. I feel like I'm in the "slow" class right now, because Mr. Chauncey is breaking every single thing down to the very basics. I could just scream! Leave me alone and let me drive!

An hour later, my wish comes true and I'm shaking like crazy with Mr. Chauncey sitting next to me in the passenger's seat. Am I really ready to drive?

"Is your cell phone off?" Mr. Chauncey asks.

"Yes."

"Did you check your mirrors?"

I look at both mirrors. "Yes."

"Do you have an inch of the car in the mirror?"

My mouth says one thing, but my face says another, prompting Mr. Chauncey to explain this whole concept of the inch-in-the-mirror theory. When he finishes taking the time to instruct me, it finally makes sense.

So far, we've stayed in the parking lot for half an hour. Then we try the street again. Mr. Chauncey's voice is soft and soothing, nothing like Miss Rebecca's mousy, panicky voice. Despite the mystery eye and the messed-up hands,

Mr. Chauncey turns out to be just the calm, collective teacher I need to get my nerves in check. Half an hour later, I feel like the queen of the road. I'm ready to tilt my seat back and go into a gangster lean as we park in the lot back at the driving school. I got this.

Jerricka is sitting on the bench waiting for her ride when the session is over. She doesn't say anything to me, and I don't say anything to her, which is just fine with me. It's big-mouth girls like her who keep up mess all the time, so I just stay away from them. I have to go back in and get a few papers, so by the time I get back to the front, she's not there anymore. Despite the chilly temperature, a few other kids and I are hanging outside waiting for rides when I see an old-school Chevy Impala pull up. It's dark outside and the windows are tinted, so I really can't see who's inside, but I can just make out one guy in the front seat. His system is so loud I think my teeth are rattling inside my head.

A few minutes later, I'm the last person left on the bench. The passenger window of the Impala rolls down, the music gets low, and I hear a voice from inside the car ask, "You need a ride?"

I'm sitting here looking all goofy and half-scared. "No, thanks." I can't really see him, but in this case it doesn't matter. My mom would not even let me breathe again if she saw me getting out of this guy's car.

"You sure?" he asks again. A few minutes later, a boy walks out of the school and gets into the Impala.

The driver makes a U-turn in the lot. Now maybe I can get a better look at his profile. I *think* he looks good, but I can't be sure. Maybe I can check him out tomorrow. I'm not getting my hopes up—not after what happened with Derrick.

My mom wants to know how the driving lesson went tonight. I tell her that things went fine. My mind really isn't on that, though. I'm wondering about the guy in the Impala. That was nice of him to offer me a ride home.

chapter eight

The next night, it's déjà vu. I'm waiting outside on the bench for my mom, when Impala boy comes for the other student again. This time, he turns off the car and gets out. My eyes almost pop out of my head. His body is slammin'—I can tell he's fine, even through a T-shirt and a denim jacket! And it just keeps getting better and better as he comes closer. This bench really isn't big enough for two strangers, but he scoots in so close that we're touching. I guess this is his idea of flirting.

"So, what's your name?" he asks.

I cut my eyes at him. He could use a little help in the how-to-approach-a-girl category, so I decide to give him a little lesson in manners. "Oh, I'm fine, how are you?"

"I can see you're *fine*, I just wanna know your name."

Okay, that was goofy. I laugh just a little, and I can see a half-grin on his face, too. I'm a sucker for dimples. "Karis."

"Karis, I'm Javon. It's nice to meet you." He holds out his hand and I shake it. His hand is warm and buttery.

"Nice to meet you, too. Now, can you please scoot over a little bit?"

He scoots in even closer to me and I push him back with my elbow, trying my best to keep from laughing out loud. "The other way!"

"Oh, I'm sorry. You gotta be more specific." He moves back and gives me some space, but I almost wish he hadn't done that, because a draft of air comes through and makes my whole body shiver.

"You cold?"

"A little. I think I'm gonna go back inside."

But before I can get up, he takes off his jacket. Out pop the muscles in his arms and chest and I'm sitting here like, *Dang, where did you get those from?* It takes me like ten seconds to stop staring at him and realize that he's offering me his jacket to stay warm. Since I'm speechless, he drapes it over my shoulders.

"Thank you, Javon." I make the mistake of looking into his face, and now I'm totally lost in his coal-black eyes. He is too cute to look at. He's got thick eyebrows, rich brown skin, and thick, kissable lips that form a perfect frame around his pearly whites. A few of his side teeth have gold trim on them, but it's not a full grill. He's got to be at least eighteen. Maybe even nineteen. What is he doing talking to me? Why on earth am I wearing his jacket? And why does it smell so good? I should take a picture of him with my cell phone.

"You need a ride home?" he asks for the second time in two days.

I shake my head. "No. My mom is on her way."

"Oh, that's my cue to go. I don't do parents." He backs off.

"Why not?"

He gives me a fake frown and says, "Parents don't like me."

"Why not?"

He raises one eyebrow and looks down at me like he's a big brother giving me some advice. "You know how your momma's always telling you to stay away from the bad crowd?"

I nod. "Yeah."

"Well, I *am* the bad crowd. All rolled into one."

I look down at his arms and notice the goose bumps. "You ain't that bad; you let me borrow your jacket when you're freezing just as much as I am. Sounds to me like something a *good* guy would do."

He puts a finger over his lips. "Shhhh. Keep that on the low-down. I've got a reputation to protect."

I roll my eyes at him. "Anyway." Then I see my mom coming into the parking lot. I practically throw Javon's jacket back at him. "Good-bye."

"Holla."

When I get into my mom's car, she's got a million questions: Who is that boy? How old is he? Why was I wearing his jacket? Are there adults supervising us after class? Why was I waiting outside instead of inside, where adults can watch over me?

She is trippin' for real! "Momma, he's just a boy who's waiting to pick up someone else. I do not know his life story!"

"Watch your mouth."

My stomach churns as I look back out of the passenger's window again. Sometimes I think I might as well go ahead and do the stuff my mom thinks I'm doing because she's gonna accuse me of doing it anyway. All I did was sit next to a boy on a bench, and she acts like I just told her I was engaged or something.

I get home and sneak to call Tamisha, telling her all about Javon. Tamisha calls Sydney, and Sydney uses her districtwide basketball connections to make a few phone calls (the Impala turns out to be a very valuable clue). Then Tamisha calls me back with everything that Sydney uncovered about Javon. He just graduated from Duncanville High School this year. He got a football scholarship to a junior college, and he actually went there over the summer but it didn't work out. Depending on who told the story, he either got kicked out for fighting or the scholarship was a joke. Now he supposedly works at Home Depot. He's also, supposedly, a dog. Somehow, that last bit of information about Javon does not surprise me. The cute ones usually are dogs because they're so used to girls giving them everything they want, and I do mean *everything*.

Well, I, for one, am not going to throw myself at Javon no matter how good he looks. If anybody's doing any throwing, it's *him*, because *he's* the one who came and sat on the bench next to *me* while I was minding my own business waiting for my ride. And *he's* the one who let me borrow his jacket while he froze his big, beautiful arms off.

Tamisha then explains to me how the *real* players do it. "They start off treating you like a lady until they get what they want. Then—BAM—they get ghost faster than a monkey in an elevator."

"What?" Her silly analogy makes me bust out laughing a little too loudly. "Why would a monkey be in an elevator?"

Tamisha laughs at herself and continues with her warning. "Look, Karis, if he's as fine as you say he is, no offense, but why else would he be coming up to you if he didn't want something from you? I mean, you're cute and everything, but let's keep it real."

"What boy in his right mind *wouldn't* like me?" I squeal. I hear my mom's door open in her bedroom. "Hold on!"

Quickly, I put the cell phone underneath the bedcovers and pull a book from my backpack. My mom knocks and opens the door in one move and finds me smiling while looking at the book.

"What you reading?"

"Just a funny story. It's for my class."

"Well, you'd better get to bed soon," she warns. "Good night."

"Good night, Momma."

Whew! That was close. I feel bad about lying to my mother, but I can't find any other way around it. Maybe if she wasn't so strict, I wouldn't *have* to lie.

I wait a few seconds, listening to my mom's house shoes walk all the way back to her bedroom door. She closes it, and I grab my cell phone again. "You still there, Tamisha?"

"Yeah. Hey! Speaking of guys liking you, I meant to tell you earlier today, I got a letter from Marlon."

Something in me jumps at the mention of Marlon's name. I guess because I pray for him every night. "How's he doing?"

"He's fine. But hey—you remember the picture we took for homecoming?"

"Yeah."

"Well, I sent it to him and he must have shown it to some of the other soldiers. He said his friend wants your address to send you a letter. You okay with that?"

I have to know. "Is he cute?"

"How am I supposed to ask my brother if another man is cute?"

I sigh. "Well, for the sake of the United States of America, I guess it doesn't matter this time."

"Aiight. I'll email him your address."

I switch the conversation back to my immediate crisis. "Okay, so you think I should leave Javon alone?"

She advises, "Well, I say go for it. Just be careful. He's probably, you know, experienced."

"How else am I supposed to get experienced if I don't have experiences?"

"You've got a point," she agrees. "I'm just saying—don't fall too hard too fast."

So, with Tamisha's blessing, I'm sitting outside in the *freezing* cold after driving lessons on Monday, hoping to see Javon again. Five minutes go by. Ten minutes go by. There's no sign of Javon, but Jack Frost is here kicking my behind, so I go back into the office suite. The guy that Javon waits for is nowhere in sight, so I give up on seeing my new friend. Fifteen minutes later, I'm the last one waiting in the driving school. I ask if I can use the office phone. Rebecca, the non-teaching teacher, tells me to hurry up because they're closing the door at 9:30 sharp.

My mom answers her cell phone and I can tell she's aggravated. "Hello?"

"Mom, it's me. Where are you?"

Out of the corner of my eye, I see Javon's Impala cruise to a stop in front of the school. My stomach suddenly fills with butterflies.

"I tried to run some errands while you were in class and

I got caught downtown. Now I'm in traffic. Somebody must have had a wreck. I'll be there in ten minutes."

I want to tell her to take her sweet time. "Well, they're gonna close the doors in five minutes."

"Go next door to the gas station and wait in there."

"Okay."

As a matter of courtesy, I feel the need to tell Javon that his friend already left. So, I throw my shoulders back and try to walk toward the door like the models on *America's Next Top Model*. My boots are topped with fur; my jeans are fitting tight; and this particular fur-lined coat always makes me look like I've got more curves than I do. I know that the wind from outside will blow my hair back as soon as I open the door and I'll really look like a model in front of Javon. I mean, I am really swingin' it. Then it happens. I don't realize the door is already locked until it's too late. *Bam!* My face hits the glass and my body bounces backwards like a broken-down yo-yo. *I cannot believe that just happened!*

I turn my back to Javon and find a seat next to the window, behind the blinds—hopefully out of his sight. I'm too embarrassed to go outside now. I'm not going *anywhere* until my momma gets here. I'm not telling Javon anything about his friend; he can wait outside all night for all I care. I turn my head a little to see if Javon is gone. He's still there. *Oh, God, if you're listening to me, please let him leave!* I cannot face him after I just looked like a bird trying to fly through a glass window.

Now here *she* comes. "I'm sorry, Karis, but I'm gonna have to lock up now. I wish I could wait with you, but my kids are with my sitter and she charges me extra if I pick them up late," Miss Rebecca says.

I roll my eyes and slur my speech. "It's okay. I'll just wait next door."

"Oh," she sighs, "you can't do that. They don't want our kids loitering in their store. But the lot is well lit and it's a pretty busy area. You'll be okay."

Old girl don't waste no time. I'm outside that door at 9:30 and two seconds. As she's locking the door, I'm standing there like I don't see Javon's car maybe four feet from me. Miss Rebecca waves good-bye and gets into her car. I take a seat on that cold, hard bench.

Javon inches the car forward a few feet until the passenger's window is right in my face. He's not laughing at me. That's a good sign. "You want to get inside?"

My mother is just going to have to get over it. If she warms my behind tonight, it will only help me thaw out faster. I hop up from the bench, open the car door, and take a seat in the front. His car smells a lot like my dad's car. I look just below the rearview mirror and see that he's got the same wintergreen odor decal that my dad has in his car. Suddenly, I feel safe and . . . well, happy, too.

Before I forget, I tell Javon, "Your friend is already gone."

"Yeah, I know. He called me a minute ago," he says. "I came to see you."

Awww . . . how sweet!

Suddenly, liquid shoots up on the windshield and the wipers swipe the window a few times. It's not raining and his view is clear, as far as I can see. "What's that for?"

"I just wanted to make sure you knew there was glass in front of you." He laughs at me finally, and I can't help but join him. I guess I deserve that one.

"Okay, okay," I give in.

"Oh, dang." He continues to laugh.

I try to explain myself through my own laughs. "The door was locked! I didn't know!"

His hand covers his stomach. "Oh, dang. That was funny than a mug."

"It would have been funnier if it wasn't me," I say as my laughter dies down.

"Aw, ain't no thang. We all . . . bump into doors . . . every now and then," he continues to joke.

"I'm getting out." I reach for the door handle, but Javon's voice stops me.

"Wait! Okay. I'm sorry, but dang. Okay, okay." He catches his breath. "I'm sorry."

And then he looks at me. The butterflies return. I can't look at him, so I look at the dashboard and down around my feet. This Impala is clean. I'll bet he doesn't allow anyone to eat in his car. Just like my daddy.

"You forgive me?" he asks.

I bite my lip to keep from smiling. "Yeah. I guess so."

We sit for another minute in silence and Javon turns on the radio. Instead of blasting the speakers, he plays "Ordinary People" softly. "You like this song?"

"It's all right."

"What kind of music do you like?"

I shrug. "All kinds. I like dance music."

"You like to dance?"

"Who doesn't?"

He raises an eyebrow. "Not me."

"Is it that you don't *like* to dance or that you *can't* dance?" I ask, looking at him now.

"I never wanted to dance."

"Mmm."

When the song goes off, the commercials come on, so Javon puts on a Jay-Z CD. "Now *that's* music," he says. "Something to ride to."

I decide to surprise him. "Is that what you do when you're not working at Home Depot?"

He sucks his neck in and squints his eyes. "How you know where I work?"

I bat my eyelashes a few times and say, "I have my sources."

"You betta watch out askin' people about me," he says. "If you want to know something about me, ask me, aiight?"

"Why you gettin' all agitated?"

He licks his lips and then says, "I just don't like people all in my business."

"You got that much business?"

"Yeah. I do."

"Fine."

A few more minutes pass, and the tension dies. Or was it passion?

"So, you need my number, right?" he asks.

"What for?"

"In case you need to ask me any more questions."

I guess that's his way of giving me his number. I gotta give it to him—he's kinda smooth. I pull out Angelique's phone and dial as he rattles off the digits. As I finish programming the number, my mom enters the parking lot.

I look at him for the second time tonight and say in all sincerity, "Thanks for letting me stay warm in your car."

"Any time, Karis."

Dang, my name sounds good when he says it.

I just know my mother is gonna go ballistic, so I try to flip the script by fussing as I get into the car, "Momma, what took you so long? Man! I was the last one here! They won't let us wait inside that gas station 'cause they don't want kids makin' trouble. For reals, it's cold out here!"

She waits until I get into my seat belt and I'm pretending to heat up my hands on the vents before she questions me. "They wouldn't let you wait in the store?"

"No, ma'am. They won't let kids from the driving school loiter. The only place I could wait was on the bench," I inform her.

"Or in the car with a boy, huh?"

Maybe a guilt trip will work. "It is cold and you were not here. I just got in the car with him—he's a nice guy, actually."

She ignores my point. "How would you know?"

"Because I talked to him," I explain.

"After you were already in the car, right?"

"I talked to him yesterday, too."

She throws her head back in a moment of sarcasm. "Two whole conversations already? Well, that changes everything!"

I can't win, so I stop talking. My mother drives out of the parking lot and we enter the flow of traffic on the highway.

Now that she has calmed down a bit, she tries to explain herself. "Karis, you can't just go hopping in every Tom, Dick, and Harry's car just because it's cold outside. There are thousands of young girls dead today because they decided to hop in the car with someone they didn't know."

"What was I supposed to do—sit on the bench and freeze to death?" I ask, careful not to let my tone approach the level of talking back.

"I'd rather see you freeze to death than have to find your body somewhere in an alley!" she reasons.

Why do parents always have to overreact and think of the worst possible scenario? I am not missing, I did not freeze, and it's not like I was on the highway hitchhiking!

"Fine. Next time, I'll just sit outside on the bench in the cold, the rain, the sleet, the snow."

My mother warns, "Watch your mouth."

I give up.

Dear Me:

Where would I be without my friend Sydney and her sister Angelique's phone? I'll tell you where I wouldn't be—I wouldn't be totally in love with one Javon Montriece Dawson. I know this whole phone thing is wrong, but my life is SOOOOO great with Javon in it. While I haven't been in his car anymore, I have definitely been talking to him almost every night. Well, let me back up—I've been so busy talking to him that I forgot to write about him in this journal!

Okay, Javon is 18 years old. He is cute, fine—all that. He drives an old Impala. He lives with his mom and his little brother, and he has a job working at Home Depot. He was in college, but he's not anymore. It's a long story. Just know that he's not stupid and he could go back to college any time he wants to. In fact, I've been trying to get him to go back and at least take a few classes. So far, I have not been successful, but I know that if I get closer to his heart, I'll be able to convince him to go back to school and maybe even come to church with me. Only time will tell!

Well, I gotta go now. It's time for church. I really don't want

to go because (since I've been using Angelique's phone) I feel
kinda guilty. I have to keep reminding myself: it's not my fault
I have to use this phone. It was just all these circumstances, you
know?
Gotta Go

> *Karis Do-What-I-Gotta-Do Reed*

We're late for service due to driver's education, so I missed
the praise and worship. As our youth pastor opens his sermon
with reference to the Twenty-third Psalm, I feel a peace come
over me. No matter how wild my life is, no matter how many
changes my mom takes me through, no matter if I'm doing
the right thing or the wrong thing, I know there's one thing
that remains the same: the Bible.

As I listen to Pastor Woodard, I begin to think of Marlon.
I wish I could record this sermon and send it to him and his
fellow soldiers. I want them to know that no matter what,
things will be fine. Even in death, things are fine for Chris-
tians because death does not have the final word.

"Young people, I want you to know that your life is not
a game. Don't play with it. Don't gamble with it. Your life
is not your own, it belongs to God," Pastor Woodard says.
I'm wondering if he's had some kind of conversation with my
mom, because this sounds a lot like her message the other
night when I got out of Javon's car. "Use your life for God's
glory. You can have fun, enjoy your life, and still do what God
wants you to do."

Now I wish I could send the tape to Javon. Sometimes he
acts like life is too short or too hard or too unfair. I don't really
know what he means by all that; I just know that life is not
supposed to revolve around trying to make money as quickly

as possible. Javon is always comparing his job at Home Depot to the money he could be making in the NFL. "They just screwed me over," he always says. I try to ask him who "they" is, and all I get from him is "the system." I try not to talk about it with him too much, because he'll get mad.

chapter nine

I am the luckiest grounded girl alive. In three and a half weeks I have managed to finish driver's ed, keep my social life (thanks to Angelique's phone), and fall in love with Javon Montriece Dawson. We haven't actually gone out yet because I'm grounded, but we do talk every day, and we did manage to see each other almost every day after driver's ed. Now, if I'm *that* productive while I'm grounded, just imagine what I can do when I get back my freedom *and* get my car for Christmas.

I shouldn't have to wait much longer to be un-grounded, though, because progress reports came today and I'm straight. Six As and two Bs. Mr. Littley, my physical education teacher, had the nerve to write the comment "Excessive Talking." Doesn't *everyone* talk excessively in PE? Teachers these days.

When my mom looks at the report, she smiles at me as I curl up next to her on the couch. I place my head in the crook between her chin and shoulder and breathe in her scent as she reads off my grades. Her body vibrates gently as she speaks. I revel in moments like this, when I get the opportunity to feel like a kid again.

"I have to give you credit," she says. "You *do* keep your grades up, if nothing else."

I slump my shoulders in disappointment and pull my head from the comfy nook. "Mo-om! You're acting like I can't do anything right except schoolwork."

She looks me in the eye. "Karis, you are so very gifted. You make friends easily, you're pretty, you've got confidence, you're smart. I just want to channel all of that in the direction God wants you to go." She puts a finger on my nose. "I pray for you every day, you know that?"

I wiggle my nose away from her. "I pray for you, too."

"Do you really?"

"Yes. I pray for you and Marlon every night."

She pulls her chin in like a drawer and looks down her nose at me. "Who's Marlon and how did he get right next to *me* on the prayer list?"

"You remember Marlon—Tamisha's brother? They're sending him to Iraq."

My mother's face falls an inch. "Oh, Lord. I didn't know that. Let me put his name on my prayer list right now." She gets up from the couch, and I grab her arm.

"Wait!"

"What?"

"Aren't you forgetting something?" I hint, but she's not getting it. "I'm still grounded."

She waves her hand at me. "Aw, girl, I thought you were really talking about something. Okay, you're no longer grounded, but don't ever let me catch you spending time at some boy's house, you hear?"

"Yes, ma'am."

I jump ahead of her and gather my cell phone, modem, and iPod from her nightstand. Honestly, being grounded is not a big deal because I usually end up doing what I want to do anyway. I'm just not crazy about all the lying I'm forced to do when I'm grounded, and I hate feeling like me and my mom are not getting along.

The first thing I do is call Javon and give him my real number. "Hey, Boo! How you doin'?"

Javon sounds surprised. "I'm good. What you up to? It ain't six yet."

"I got my real phone back. You got the number in your ID?"

"Yeah, I gotcha."

I love it when he says that.

"You at work?"

"Naw." He hesitates. "I got fired."

"How? What happened?"

"It's a long story," he says with an evasive laugh.

"I'm listening."

He makes a sound like air coming out of a balloon. "Look, I'm just gonna tell you the truth, 'cause it ain't no need in lyin' to you. Me and this cat who works there had a little side business goin' at the store."

I still don't get it. "What?"

"Say we get fifteen ceiling fans in on the truck. We scan in twelve and sell the other three for cash."

It finally clicks. "Javon, are you saying that you were stealing?"

"No, no, no," he sings in baritone. "Intentional miscalculation."

I think about it for a second. "Same thing."

Then he goes into this story about how all the guys are doing it, but they only fired the minorities and the young ones. The shift managers who were in on it just got written up for not reporting the shortage of inventory. "But, for real, *they're* the ones that turned *me* onto it."

I cannot believe my man was stealing. "Javon, why did you do that? I mean, you had a job and now you've got nothing."

"I'll get another job," he assures me.

"Would you *please* not steal at your new job?" I'm shaking my head now.

He makes that blowing sound again. "Look, people do it every day. The next man they hire will get his hustle on, too."

"Just because somebody *else* is stealing doesn't mean *you* have to steal."

"They were probably gonna fire me anyway right after Christmas. But check it—I told you from the beginning: I ain't perfect, so don't be doin' all this preachin', okay? Sometimes things just happen. Everybody doesn't live in a perfect little world like you."

My mouth drops open. This isn't the first time he has accused me of being a Little Miss Priss, and I don't appreciate him putting off his problems on me. "My world is not perfect, for your information. My parents are divorced, my mom is workin' mad hours to pay the bills, she gets on my nerves, and I have to work hard in school to keep my grades up."

He waits for a second. "Is that it?"

"What you mean, *is that it?*"

"If your parents getting divorced, you having to go to

school, and your mom trying to be a good mom while she works is the worst thing happening in your life, you got it easy." He dismisses me with another laugh. "I wish I had *your* problems."

He is saved by an incoming call and says he has to get back with me later. It's a good thing we have to hang up right now, because I'm fuming. In the first place, he has no business stealing and getting fired. And now he wants to act like he's got it so hard and I've got it so easy. *Whatever!*

I go ahead and do my homework and watch a little television while I'm waiting for his call. Then I figure I'd better call Tamisha and Sydney before they start accusing me of neglecting them for a man. I tell Tamisha about Javon stealing and she says this is definitely a bad sign. "My daddy says that if a person will lie, they'll steal, and if they'll steal, they'll kill."

"Javon did *not* lie to me, and he is *not* going to kill me. He's just a onetime . . . embezzler," I take up for him.

"Well, if you want a jailbird for a boyfriend, that's on you. Just don't leave him with your purse, girl." She smacks and says slowly, "Keep the purse with you at all times."

I can almost see Tamisha's lips moving in slow motion, and it's actually kind of funny. "Don't talk about my future husband."

"How he gon' be your husband when he gon' be in jail?" She laughs.

Sydney is next on my list of people to call. I'm thinking that maybe I shouldn't tell her about Javon getting fired, but she'll find out sooner or later through Tamisha anyway. Sydney, future lawyer that she is, wants to know all the specifics of Javon's case. "Was he caught on tape? Was it entrapment? Did he confess?"

"I don't know all that, Sydney," I tell her. "He said that only the ones on the bottom of the food chain got fired."

"Sounds like racial and age discrimination to me. He was influenced and corrupted by his older white superiors who perhaps coerced him into—"

"Sydney! He's already fired."

"Does he want the job back?"

"No. He's gonna find another one."

"Well," she offers her best free legal advice, "tell him to stop stealin'."

"Okay," I agree.

"And could you please get a picture of this guy, 'cause you sure are lowering the standards to be with him," she offers as another piece of advice that I didn't ask her for. "He'd better look *real* good."

I assure her, "Trust me. He's worth it."

I don't have to worry about Javon calling, unlike some other guys. It might be an hour, two hours, or three hours, but Javon always calls me back. In the meantime, I help my mom with dinner in the kitchen. We're making Hamburger Helper, a green salad, and corn. Actually, she wants to mix corn in with the Hamburger Helper and make what she calls "goolosh," but I tell her that with a name like "goolosh," it must be nasty. She laughs like crazy and calls Grandma Ruthie in Philadelphia to tell her what I said. I haven't talked to my grandma in a while, so my mom puts her on the phone.

"Hey, Pookie, how you doin'?" My grandmother is the only one who still calls me that.

"I'm fine, Grandma Ruthie. How are you?"

I don't know why I asked that question. She spends the next ten minutes telling me how her arthritis is acting up, how she's been having lots of gas, and how she almost fell getting out of the shower three months ago so she bought some nonslip disks for the tub. "Other than that, I'm fine," she sings now. I answer a few questions about school and then politely say good-bye to her. I give the phone back to my mom. The more my grandmother talks, the more my mom makes faces. I'm looking at my mom and thinking this is exactly how I feel when *she* goes on and on about nothing.

After dinner, I watch a little more television, take my shower, do my homework, and get my clothes ready for the next day. Derrick calls. I think he's mad at me, because we haven't talked since the night I went over to his house.

"So what's up? We still together or what?" he questions me.

"Derrick, we were never *together*. We are friends—I told you that."

"Oh, we're *friends* now?"

"Yes! We always *were* friends."

Next thing I know, he's cussing me out like I owe him some money! Now, I'm not really good at cussing, but I can't go out like that! I think about letting a few four-letter words roll off my tongue, but they just don't sound right coming from my mouth, so I let Derrick meet Mr. Click. When he calls back, I reject his call both times.

chapter ten

Forget Derrick. Forget Quinten (for now). Forget all these other guys, because I've got my hands full with Javon. I call Tamisha and tell her what just happened with Derrick. We both laugh. Boys can be so crazy sometimes. My phone beeps, and I know who it is before I even look at the screen. "I gotta go. It's Javon."

"Yeah, you better answer it," Tamisha laughs. "This might be his one phone call."

"Ha, ha. Very funny."

"Audi."

Javon is almost whispering when I answer the phone. "What you doin'?"

"I'm about to go to bed," I tell him. "Why are you whispering?"

"Because I'm right in front of your house."

I smack one good time. "Quit playin', Javon. You don't even know where I live."

"I know what street you live on and I know what kind of car your mom drives," he lets me know. "I want to see you tonight."

I still don't believe him.

"Is that your light on in that room right next to the driveway?"

"My window is next to my driveway, but that is irrelevant at the moment. You need to go on home and go to sleep so you can get up early tomorrow to find another job," I tell him.

That's when I notice that I'm hearing my neighbor's dog bark outside and on the phone at the same time. I hear a tap at my window. "Javon!" I whisper-yell into the phone. I raise the blinds and pull the curtain back. Javon is standing outside my window! My face is a big O as he helps me lift up the window. The adrenaline is pumping through my veins, and I hope like crazy that my mom doesn't come out of her room, because I will have to crawl out this window to go live with Javon forever if she does. The only reason I'm even opening this window now is because I know my mom is working an early shift tomorrow and she usually goes to bed pretty early under those circumstances.

"Javon, what are you doing here?" I whisper.

"I wanted to see you."

"You can't *be* here, Javon. Are you trying to get me killed?"

He smiles. "Calm down, girl. It's cool."

I look at him for a moment and give my heart a chance to slow its pace. I weigh the facts: my mom is asleep, and all he's doing is standing at my window. He's not actually *in* my house; we're just talking, same as if we were on a cell phone. Okay, I've talked my heart rate into slowing down now.

"Wait!" I look around for my cell phone and realize that it's still in my hand. This is crazy, but I must keep my priorities in order. "I've got to take a picture—me and you. Smile." I reach through the window and pull him closer. I count to three and snap the shot, hoping this won't be the last known photograph of me. Well, if it is, at least Tamisha and Sydney will know what Javon looks like.

When I look at the photo, I see that Javon didn't smile. "Why didn't you show your teeth?"

"I only smile on my mug shots."

"Stop it, Javon. You do not have any mug shots."

"How you think I knew how to open your window from outside just now?" he asks.

I fidget just a bit because he apparently really is a pro at opening windows from the wrong side.

"Practice, baby. Practice."

"Anyway. You are not a burglar, Javon."

He cracks a smile. "You're right. But I have stolen a car or two. You wanna go for a ride in that Benz down the street?"

"No, I do not." I dismiss his suggestion, wondering if he is kidding about this, too.

Javon looks past me into my bedroom now and sees a sea of hot pink. "Dang, girl, what you got going on in this bedroom? It's pink galore up in here."

I lean to the side so that he can take in the view. My room is pretty, if I don't say so myself. I only wish that it were a little cleaner right about now. My jeans are lying on the floor, and I've got a pair of shoes that I need to put away.

"You ain't got no pictures of no other dudes up in here, do you?" he asks.

I squint my eyes and answer, "No."

"You'd better not," he says as his beautiful eyes return to mine.

We talk for a few more minutes about where he's going to look for a job tomorrow. We also finish the conversation we started earlier. I have to agree that my life is easier than his. Javon's father was a truck driver who died in an accident when Javon was ten years old. I knew that, but until tonight I had never seen the look in Javon's eyes when he talked about his father. Yeah, Javon has had it harder than me.

Javon makes a sudden move to scratch his leg, and my neighbor's German shepherd, who has been sitting on his behind and present throughout the whole conversation, barks again. "I'd better quit while I'm ahead, Javon. My mom could come in here any minute. I forgot to tell you earlier—I just got off punishment. I don't want to mess it up again."

"For real? So we can go kick it now?"

I'm thinking about Javon pulling up in my driveway with his gold-rimmed teeth and that Impala. I really don't know if my mom will let me go out with him. "I've gotta ask my mom."

"Cool. But like I said—moms don't like me. So if she says no, we'll just have to find a way around it."

The thought of sneaking around with Javon is somewhat enticing. Really, this whole conversation is rather exciting. Javon smiles again, and I might just melt into the windowsill. This is perfect—like Romeo and Juliet. The moonlight shining above us, the brisk night air making my cheeks all rosy, the glisten of his gold teeth. I'm really not all that crazy about guys with any type of gold in their mouths, but I'm feelin' Fantasia right now. A hood boy will do me just fine. Yep, this is just like Shakespeare, and now all of a sudden I'm feeling lovey-dovey. This would be a perfect night for our first kiss. "Javon, can I have a kiss?"

"Oh, no can do." He steps back.

I stand up a bit, accidentally bumping my head on the window. "Ow!" I cover my mouth with my hand.

"Shhh!" he teases.

"Why won't you kiss me?" I whisper, rubbing the top of my head.

He stops and looks at me like a kid looking through the window at a bakery. "I don't want to start something we can't finish."

I figure I'm pretty safe inside my bedroom, so I press the issue. "You mean, you can't just give me an innocent little kiss?"

"There's no such thing as an innocent kiss with me."

When he says that, I get a funny feeling in my stomach— like when you're going downhill on a roller coaster, only it kind of tickles. Suddenly, I have to agree with Javon. We'd better not kiss tonight.

It's time for me to go to my dad's again. I'm looking forward to it, but I know I won't have nearly as much time to talk to Javon. To celebrate the fact that I passed my driving test exactly two hours ago, Shereese has a weekend of shopping planned for us. Who am I to disappoint the girl?

We hop into her Honda, blast the stereo on R&B, and take off for some well-deserved retail therapy. In the mall, I'm noticing how all these guys are flirting with us. That never happens when I'm with my mom. I mean, boys look at me, but I'm off limits when I go somewhere with her. When I'm with

Shereese, however, I'm available. I meet one guy while we are at the Gap. He works there, and he asks me for my number while Shereese is standing right next to me! It's amazing. I must shop with her more often.

I also appreciate the fact that Shereese lets me get things that my mom would look at and say, *"Wait until you're a little older."* Well, I *am* older. The last time I shopped with my mom, I was fifteen. I'm sixteen now. This red leather miniskirt should be fine . . . I hope.

When Shereese and I finish shopping, we meet my dad at Cheddar's restaurant. As soon as we finish eating, my dad has a big surprise for me. There is a car lot right next to the restaurant. We hop the railing between the two businesses, and I am in heaven. I can't believe it! We are actually looking at cars! My dad makes it clear to the salesman that he's just looking for something to get me around the Metroplex with no problem. The salesman takes us to "cash cars," as he calls them. There's not much to choose from, but I do see a cute little Toyota Corolla and a Ford Escort. My dad takes the salesman's card and says, "I'll get back to you."

I bounce all the way back to my dad's SUV. "Are you gonna call him? When are you gonna get it?"

"I've gotta talk to Santa first," he teases. Shereese is in the front, and she's smiling, too.

I cannot contain myself. "For Christmas, right?"

"I have to check things out, Karis. You don't just buy a used car without doing your homework. You have to check the value and get a certified mechanic to look at it. Actually, you can help me out. I want you to look up the Kelley Blue Book value on those cars that we looked at today and tell me what they're worth."

I don't know a blue book value from a red book value, and I sure don't know who Kelly is, but I somehow get the feeling that google.com will be my best friend when it comes to this car business. "Okay."

When I get back to my mom's house later that day, I call Javon and give him the news. He's excited for me and tells me that he can get me a hookup on a sound system. I give him a big kiss through the phone as a form of thanks. Sydney calls and I send her to voice mail. She can wait. Or can she? She calls back again. And again.

"Hey, let me call you back, Javon. This is my girl Sydney."

"Later."

I switch lines, and Sydney's panicked voice comes through the phone with painstaking clarity. "Karis, we've got a *big* problem. I mean *huge*!"

"What?"

"I got the mail today. I'm looking at the family phone bill, and the bill from Angelique's phone alone is like nine hundred dollars!"

"Nine hundred dollars! What are you talking about? I didn't make any phone calls before six!" I exclaim truthfully, trying to remember to breathe.

"Well, I don't know what happened," Sydney stumbles. Her voice begins to crack. "I . . . I thought she and I had the same plan. I guess I was wrong about the time or something. I don't know. All I know is, Angelique's phone bill is nine hundred forty-two dollars and seventy-three cents, Karis. What are we gonna do? My parents are gonna kill me!"

I'm thinking. "Have your parents seen the bill yet?"

"No."

"How long until it's due?"

"We've got ten days—probably five until my dad goes online and views it. He's serious about keeping up with bills. Dang, Karis, did you have to talk on the phone every day to 555-3877?" she starts with the accusations. "Who is that, anyway?"

I'm wondering why that's important, but I answer, "Javon."

"Javon the *jailbird*?"

"He is *not* a jailbird."

"Ooh, I can't believe you are stupid enough to run up nine hundred dollars in phone bills talking to a thuggish thief," she judges my man under her breath. "And by the way—he did not look all that cute on the picture you sent us."

I'm ready to reach through this phone and pop her one good time. "*You* are the one who told me not to use the phone until after six p.m., so don't blame it on me, okay?"

"You're the one who was grounded in the first place! You shouldn't have been on the phone anyway!" she yells.

To clear the record, I yell back, "It was *your* idea, remember?"

"I never would have let you use the phone if I had known you were gonna get hooked up with a hoodlum—"

"Don't hate 'cause you ain't got no man to talk to! Maybe if you quit hangin' around all them basketball girls, you might get a chance to actually meet somebody."

"Oh, I know you didn't just say that!"

"Yes, I did!" I didn't really mean what I was saying, but what else was I supposed to do? How she just gon' blame this nine-hundred-dollar bill all on me? And why does she have to bring Javon into it? Well, two can play dirty.

"I bet you won't say that crap to my face!" Sydney warns.

"I bet you won't be gettin' nine hundred dollars from me, either. This is *your* fault, Sydney, not mine!"

"This is what I get for tryin' to help a friend, huh?" She smacks her lips.

I feel a pang of guilt, but I'm too mad to give in to it right now. "I guess so."

Now Sydney starts crying as she brings in the *serious* dramatics. "You know what? Forget you, Karis. And don't give me no more prayers to pray, talking about God and all that, okay? 'Cause what kinda church you go to where you can run up my sister's phone bill talkin' to a thief and then don't wanna have nothin' to do with me when I'm tryin' to figure out what to do because I was tryin' to help *your* behind, okay?" And she hangs up in my face.

Okay, I know I'm wrong about some of this, but I'm not all wrong. She's the one who told me it was okay to talk after six. Still. What she just said about God, church, and prayer really bugs me. I don't want Sydney to think bad about God and church because of what I say or do. *Why did she have to bring God into it?* Now everything is different.

Dear Me:
How is it that my life can go from happiness to total stank in less than sixty seconds?

Karis Why-Me Reed

chapter eleven

I'm barely in the school when Tamisha comes up to me with an outright attitude. She's wearing a ponytail this week—colors 1B and 32. She'll probably be wearing earth tones and black until we're released for Christmas vacation this Friday.

I don't have to ask. She has already talked to Sydney. I'm really not trying to hear Tamisha right now, but I kind of need to see whose side she's on, so I wait for her to talk. "Karis, think about it. What would you do if you were in Sydney's shoes?" she quizzes me as we wait in the cafeteria for the first bell to ring. I don't usually eat breakfast at school, but those cinnamon rolls do call a sister every once in a while. Tamisha is following me through the line, and when we get to the front, the cafeteria lady fusses because Tamisha isn't supposed to be in line unless she buys something. Tamisha picks up a carton of orange juice and pays for it so the lady won't call the cafeteria police.

We find a table and Tamisha offers me the juice. I take it from her with thanks.

Tamisha continues the conversation. "How would you feel if you were Sydney right now?"

"I wouldn't *be* Sydney right now because if I let her use *my* phone I would tell her the *right* time to use it," I explain.

Tamisha reasons, "You *know* she made a mistake. There's no way she would have given you the wrong time on purpose."

"Look, it's not like I don't want to help her, but I don't have nine hundred dollars, and neither does my mom. If I had it, I would give it to her in a heartbeat—you know that."

"What about your dad?"

"He ain't got no money either." Suddenly it occurs to me that he *does* have money—for my car. *Oh no! There is no way.* I don't even know why that thought bothered to pop into my mind.

"Well, you know what her parents are gonna say." Tamisha sighs.

"What?"

"They're gonna tell Sydney that it's her responsibility, since she was the one who gave the phone to you," Tamisha spoke the truth. Sydney's always talking about how her dad is into "personal responsibility." And every time she says those two words, she holds up the quotation mark sign and rolls her eyes.

My cinnamon roll loses its taste because Tamisha keeps talking about this problem. She just made me waste $1.25. I'm not looking at her. I keep my eyes focused on the courtyard just beyond the window, and I'm suddenly thinking about how stupid I must have looked when I walked into that door at driver's ed. It makes me laugh out loud.

"What's so funny?" Tamisha asks, agitated.

"I was just thinking about the time I embarrassed myself in front of Javon." I forgot to tell Tamisha about the incident. From the look on her face, she does not want to hear it now.

"You wouldn't be with Javon if it weren't for Sydney. It's only because of her phone that you two were able to talk and get to know each other better. Have you thought about that?" Tamisha raises an eyebrow and sets her dark brown eyes on me.

Did she have to say that? She makes it sound like hundreds of years after me and Javon get married, our kids and grand-kids will owe all their happiness to Sydney.

"Are you going to even *ask* your mom for the money?" she continues.

I almost choke on the juice. The thought of telling my mother is ridiculous. "I can't tell my mom about it because then she'll know that I was on the phone the whole time I was supposed to be grounded, and then I'll get *re*-grounded and . . . pshhhh . . . then I don't know *what's* gonna happen to me."

"Well, make up another reason," Tamisha suggests as she pinches off a piece of my cinnamon roll.

"What could I tell my mother that would make her give me nine hundred dollars that she does *not* have?"

"How 'bout four-fifty? Maybe you and Sydney could split it," Tamisha tries to negotiate. "We've been friends for a long time. I know you two can work something out."

"What did Sydney say? Does she want to go half-and-half?"

"I haven't asked her, but I'm just saying. It's a lot better than nine hundred for one person, right?"

I shake my head as I eat the last of my breakfast. "We can say we're going to split it all day, but it's not gonna make any difference because I don't have four hundred fifty dollars, either. What part of 'I'm broke' don't you understand?"

The bell rings and I'm so happy to be getting away from Tamisha that I don't know what to do. Before I started talking to her, I was doing a very good job of avoiding my guilt. Now she's brought friendship and Javon into it. Things are getting more complicated. When I go to the bathroom between classes, I can barely look at myself in the mirror. My mom's eyes are screaming at me like crazy.

We're on a B-day schedule, so I don't have any classes with Sydney or Tamisha today. I think Sydney's got an away game tomorrow, so there's a good chance that I won't see her then, either. After that, we've got exams, so it's possible that I won't have to see Sydney until Thursday—the last day of classes before Christmas break. I figure I can ignore her until after I get my car, and when I get the car, I will get a job for a few weeks and pay back the money. Plus I will take Sydney anywhere she wants to go for a whole year, assuming that she will still be my friend, which is questionable.

My mom knows something is up. She's asked me twice today already if something is wrong, and I keep telling her no. Javon says I'm not talking much tonight and he wants to know what my problem is. I go ahead and tell him about the bill. He says a few cuss words in response to the amount. Then he offers his apologies. "Dang, Karis. Well . . . if I had a job, I'd try to help you out. But you know my situation right now."

It's really sweet of him to want to help. That's my boo! We've got a date planned for Friday night. I haven't actually asked my mom if I can go. For the last couple of days, I have been dropping Javon's name here and there so when I do ask her for permission to go out, it won't be a total surprise. Javon won't be my first date, but he will be the first one whose parents my mom does not know. So far, I have only had two official pick-me-up-and-go-out dates—with Henry Blevins and Antwone Jarr. Both of them go to my church. They were okay, I guess. No sense of adventure. Both of them are just like me, and that's pretty boring for a boy.

My unofficial dates, however, started when Tamisha got a car over the summer. One time Tamisha, Sydney, and I met up with three other guys at the movies. Really, it was no different from when I went out with Henry. It just seemed more exciting because we weren't supposed to be there with them. The other unofficial dates have been a matter of meeting up at a dance, at the mall, or someplace like that.

Javon says that we should go to a drive-in movie. I'm like, "That's from the fifties." Plus it's supposed to be pretty cold Friday night.

When I mention the weather to Javon, he brags, "Don't worry. I'll keep you warm."

Then I get that crazy roller-coaster-tickle feeling again and I start giggling like I'm in the second grade. Sometimes I feel so childish when we're talking. Javon will be nineteen in a few months. I hope he won't think I'm too young for him then.

Sydney hasn't called me all week. No doubt she can't talk on the phone, and her parents probably really are holding her personally responsible. I do feel bad about this, and I hope that someday we can be friends again. I know my momma doesn't have the money, though, so what else can I do? There's no sense in *both* of us being eternally grounded. I have passed Sydney a few times in the hallway, but I can't look at her. Tamisha is acting funny, too. So all week at school I've just been going to class and trying to study for exams while trying to think of a way to approach my mom about going out with Javon.

By Wednesday, I know I'd better say something about this upcoming date. On the way back from midweek service at church, I am finally sitting in the car with my mom, and we're having a pretty deep conversation. She says she hopes I have enough sense not to live with a man unless we're *married*. I guess this is her way of telling me that my dad is doing the wrong thing with Shereese. "Your father is an adult and he has the God-given right to make choices. I'm just letting you know: this particular choice does not line up with God's best for a relationship between a man and a woman. You understand?"

"Yes, ma'am."

"No, do you *really* understand?" She beats her hand on the steering wheel with each syllable.

I bug my eyes out and look at her. "Yes, I understand."

"Then what am I saying?" she asks, sticking her lips out.

"You're saying my dad is making an ungodly choice by living with Shereese, and you hope that I will not make that same choice when I grow up." There. I just summarized it for her. Mrs. Clawson would be proud.

My mom takes a deep breath. Her oily skin shines from the lights on the dashboard. Her skin always shines at the end of the day as her makeup wears off. I wonder why she won't put on more makeup, but her eyes tell the story. She's tired. "Okay. You're getting the picture. Now, I don't need you to go back and tell your daddy that I said he's livin' in sin. This conversation is between me and you, just like what he does is between him and God."

"Yes, ma'am." I figure this would be a good time to spring the date with Javon on her.

"Momma, you know that boy named Javon that I've been telling you about?" I ask in my most casual tone.

"The one with the ghetto-mobile, from the driving school?"

I'm glad she remembers him. "Yes, that's him. Well, anyway, he asked me to go out with him on Friday . . . and I told him I didn't know . . . so . . . I was just wondering if I could go." Now I'm fidgeting in my seat. Not exactly the best proposal.

My mom sighs again, like she thinks I'm making the same bad choices as my dad. She's kind of making me mad being so judgmental. I mean, Javon's car is old, and a lot of questionable guys might drive old Impalas, but Javon's car used to be his father's. After his father died, Javon's uncle drove it until Javon turned eighteen. Javon loves that car. He has put a lot of work into it, and it means a lot to him.

"Where y'all plannin' on goin'?" At least she's asking.

"To a movie and probably to get something to eat."

My mom thinks about it for a few minutes. Maybe I should say something. No, I'd better not. Sometimes when I start to add information to help her make a decision, my mom ends up using the information against me. It wouldn't take much for her to deny this request, so I keep my mouth shut.

She cuts her eyes at me one good time. She relents. "Karis, I've spent the last sixteen years teaching you right from wrong. I'm going to trust that you would not be dating him if he wasn't half decent. Make sure he knows to come *inside* when he picks you up, and make sure you're home by eleven or you will *not* be seeing him again."

Inside, my heart is racing and I'm singing, *"Go Karis! It's my birthday! Go! Go! Go! Break it down now!"* All I mumble to my mom is, "Okay."

chapter twelve

I can't wait to get in and call Javon. He's not answering his phone, which is weird. Maybe he found a job or something. I leave him a message and get ready for bed. I remember to pray for my mom and for Marlon. I thank God that my mom is going to let me go out with Javon. The situation with Sydney comes to mind. I don't really know what to pray, so I say, "Lord, please help in this problem that me and Sydney are having."

An hour later, Javon still hasn't called. I'm not worried. I log into myspace.com and send out a few shouts to my cyber-friends, the only friends I have left at this point. Another hour passes, and I decide to go to sleep knowing that Javon will call me when he gets the chance—whether it is in two minutes or two hours. I fall asleep with my phone beside me.

* * *

I just woke up, and I cannot believe that Javon did not call me back! Okay, I'm calling him again. Where was he and what was he doing last night? I leave another message and start getting ready for school, keeping the phone with me as I go back and forth between my bedroom and the bathroom. He still hasn't called! Now I've made it all the way to school and I am ready to blow. I'm also scared because I hope nothing has happened to him. Oh my gosh. If Javon died, I would fall apart. My one true love, gone before we even went out on a date. The thought brings tears to my eyes until I realize that I'm walking into Mrs. Clawson's room. Sydney should be here any moment. I try to put potential grief aside to deal with this hostile situation.

I go to my seat and pull out my pencils for the test. I'm reviewing my notes when Sydney and Tamisha walk in together. Tamisha's desk is to my right, and Sydney's is on the other side of Tamisha's. They take their seats and carry on with the conversation that they must have been having before they walked inside the classroom. They don't even look at me. Tamisha laughs a little, and I'm feeling like a total outsider. I make the mistake of looking toward them, and my eyes meet up with Sydney's.

"Whatch-u lookin' at?" She rolls her neck to one side and I see her eyebrows scrunch up in the middle. I really am not in the mood for this, so I look back down at my notes. "That's what I thought."

She's really asking for it, but I don't want to get into it with Sydney because, number one, we are friends. Number two, Sydney lifts weights. I ignore her completely, and when the bell rings, bringing Mrs. Clawson into the room, I am relieved. Tamisha's just sitting there like she's all innocent in this. I know Tamisha doesn't like to be in the middle of mess, but how is she my friend when she won't even talk to me? I see whose friend she *really* is. Maybe she was never my friend in the first place.

No. I'm only kidding myself. We've had some good times together. Sixth-grade prom, middle-school crushes, the time when her mom got sick and Tamisha and Marlon lived with us for a week while her parents went out of town to see a specialist. Sydney and I used to have to write sentences all the time for talking too much in class. All three of us almost got killed together when Sydney convinced us that dog-paddling was a natural human skill and we almost drowned at the community pool. Yes, we have been through a lot, and now it looks like I may have to start over with a new set of friends.

I don't want new friends. I want Tamisha and Sydney, but how am I supposed to get them back without nine hundred dollars—or at least four hundred and fifty? Mrs. Clawson is up at her desk trying to make sure that she has enough exams for us all. In the meantime, my eyes are starting to sting from the tears that I'm trying to blink back. My two best friends are mad at me, and I have no way of making things better.

I rip off a corner of paper from my notes and write the only thing that might help: *I'm sorry,* I tap Tamisha on the shoulder, and she slowly turns her head to look at me. I whisper, "Give this to Sydney."

Tamisha takes the note from me and passes it. I watch Sydney read it. She takes a deep breath and writes something. When it gets back to me, I open it and read: *Sorry won't pay the bill.*

I whisper across Tamisha, "I don't *have* the money, Sydney!"

She lowers her head and answers back, "Have you even asked your mom?"

"No! I don't want to get in even more trouble!"

Sydney's eyes are watering now as we both lean in toward Tamisha's desk. "You have no idea what trouble is! My dad is gonna pay this bill, but I have to pay him back. You know how I have to pay him back?"

I slowly shrug my shoulders.

Sydney's voice is escalating out of her control. "I have to get a *job* next summer, which means I cannot go to basketball camp, which means I won't be able to up my game before my junior year, which means I may not be getting into the W-N-B-A because of Y-O-U!"

I try to calm her. "Sydney, I can get a job as soon as I get a car—"

"Mighty funny how you got money for a *car* but you ain't got no money to help pay this *phone* bill," she cuts me off as she wipes away a loose tear.

Though Tamisha is shorter than me, somehow it seems like she's looking down at me. I try to explain myself to both of them. "I have been waiting my whole life for a car and you know it!"

"*I've* been waiting *my* whole life to play pro basketball. You know the scouts really start looking at you during your junior year. If I spend the summer flippin' burgers, I will not be on top of my game when the season starts. But you know what? I ain't gonna worry about it, Karis. What goes around comes around. And you better hope I don't see *you* without one of these *teachers* around."

By this time, the people around us are getting sucked into the drama, and I hear a soft "oooooh" in the room. Mrs. Clawson calls out, "Settle down, class. Settle down. I'll give you a few more minutes to look through your notes."

Tamisha tries to calm the situation. "Y'all, we've been friends—"

"She ain't my *friend*," Sydney states. "What kind of *friend* would leave another *friend* hanging like this?"

Tamisha blows out all the air in her lungs and takes turns looking at both of us.

Sydney and I are back in our places now. I hear a sniffle coming from her every couple of minutes. Before I know it, I'm crying, too, and I can hardly concentrate on my test. I'm guessing on the last ten questions because I can't take it anymore. I turn in the exam and lay my head down on my desk for the rest of the period. While I'm sitting here thinking, the words that my pastor preached on Wednesday night are coming to me. He talked about forgiveness. I'm talking to the little guilt-voice in my head: *Sydney is the one who needs to forgive. Not me. Besides, I already said I was sorry. What else am I supposed to do?* The answer pops into my head like a lightbulb: *Help.*

When the bell rings and my two ex-friends leave the room without me, I know what must be done. I have to tell my mom. Hopefully, she will forgive me, and hopefully she and I can help resolve this issue without getting my dad or the car money involved. I might get re-grounded, but what good is being off groundation if you don't have friends? I will tell my mom first thing *after* my date with Javon.

Today is one of those days when I'm so glad my mom isn't home. If she were here, she'd pull the whole truth out of me with one of those "I can tell there's something wrong with you and I'm not budging until you spill the beans" lines. My mom went almost five months without telling my grandmother that she was pregnant with me, so my mom rarely lets anything go without getting to the bottom of it.

I don't feel like riding home with Tamisha today. The bus ride is terribly loud, but it is preferable to the icy-cold silent treatment I'm sure Tamisha would have given me. Even though she's trying really hard to remain partial, it's not working. I know she's on Sydney's side, and that hurts. My stop is the third one on the route. I exit the bus and stop at the mailbox to retrieve the bills. As a matter of habit, I thumb through them just to make sure there's nothing for me.

Surprise! Surprise! I've got a letter from Marlon. *Marlon? Why is Marlon writing me?* Well, it must be the letter from his soldier friend, I'm guessing. I rush to the house, squirming on the inside, and fumble through my purse to find my keys. I push open the door, throw my backpack on the floor (a luxury I can only afford when my mom is at work), secure the entry, and rush to my bedroom to read the letter. *Could this be the guy of my dreams? Could he be the one?* Well, first things first: what's his name?

I open the envelope carefully so that I can salvage the address and then read a letter that completely blows my mind:

Hi Karis,

It's me—Marlon. I know I said I had a "friend" who wanted to talk to you, but I had to find some kind of way to get around Tootie and get to you myself. Sorry I lied ☺. I know you're probably wondering why I'm writing you. To tell the truth, I'm wondering that same thing myself. I've known you for all these years and I never thought of you as anyone other than Tootie's friend until recently. When I took a good look at the picture of Tootie and you, it occurred to me: she's not a little kid anymore, and neither are you. Tootie also told me that you are praying for me every day. That means so much to me—you just don't know. I grew up going to church and hearing about God. Times like these, I really do need someone to keep my name in God's ear because it is CRAZY over here. There are things happening here that you'll never see on TV. Things I can't even write about in this letter.

Well, I just wanted to say "thanks" for praying for me. The first six weeks I was here, I got letters from several females talking about how they loved me and wanted to be with me—but not one of them offered to pray for me every day.

I hope I'm not making you too uncomfortable by asking you to write me back. You can tell Tootie if you want, I don't mind. She writes me, too, but she's my sister. I could really use a friend from back home right now—one who isn't just trying to write me because I used to play basketball or because I was prom king. One who cares enough to pray for me every day . . .

I understand if you're too busy to write. I remember how hard it was to keep up with friends & grades. If you'd like, you can just send me an email (marlon.banks@mil.gov), although an email message can't be packed up and carried around like a letter ☺. Remember, if this is just too weird for you, I understand that, too. No worries. Just take my "thanks" and keep praying for me, please.

Sincerely,
—Marlon Banks

Whoa! Is he trying to flirt with me? I gotta read that again!
OMG! Again!

I smother myself with a pillow and scream like crazy! Marlon Banks wants *me* to write him! Why did he have to wait until he was in the line of fire before he could see how perfectly matched we are? We have the same background, the same values, we love the same people. Yes! Yes! Who can I call? Can't call Sydney or Tamisha. Certainly can't tell Javon. I can't call anybody else at my school because the news will make it back to Tamisha. Dang! I can't tell anyone!

I cannot keep this all bottled up inside myself or I'll explode. My only hope is my online friends. I power up my computer and send out an SOS to a few of my myspace.com contacts. I catch seven of my friends online. We open up a chat and I share what's going on with Marlon. Four of them say go for it. Two say that I should talk to Tamisha first. One asks if I already have a boyfriend. It takes me a moment to come back down to earth and remember that the answer to this question is yes. How could I have forgotten about my boo so quickly? What kind of person forgets about the love of her life because an old crush comes into the picture?

Since I confess to having a boyfriend already, the online vote changes. Two say go for it. Two say forget about Marlon because it puts my current relationship with Javon and possibly my friendship with Tamisha in jeopardy, especially since I'm a "player," as they put it. One says forget about Javon because he'll always be here but Marlon may not, and I should seize the moment. The last two say that I should keep my options open by just letting everyone know the truth.

That's just the thing: I don't really know what the truth is. Yes, I'm crazy about Marlon. Yes, I'm in love with Javon. No, I don't want to be at odds with Tamisha, but since I already am, there's no way I can talk this out with her right now. She might even tell Marlon the situation with Sydney from their point of view, and then he'll think I'm some kind of traitor.

No. I'm not telling anybody anything until I can figure out a better plan. I'll keep it all to myself. I just hope I don't explode.

I open my spiral, tear out a sheet of paper, and get my mind prepared to write Marlon back. Where do I start? I suppose I could start with the truth, the whole truth, and nothing but the truth:

Dear Marlon,

I had the biggest crush on you two years ago. I cannot believe you wrote me! Are you trying to flirt with me? I hope so, because you are so cute and fine! I cannot wait until you send me a picture so I can buy a photo frame key ring and put your picture in it! I know Tamisha (oh, I forgot—you call her Tootie) will probably not like this whole thing, but seriously, this is like a dream come true for me. I do pray for your protection and your sanity. When you come home, I will be sooo happy!

No. That's stupid and immature. Marlon will think I'm desperate and flaky. He will wish he'd never written me and he'll think that I'm still a little girl. I ball up the first draft, take a deep breath, and try to think like an eighteen-year-old. I dash toward my closet and hop up to the shelf to retrieve my thesaurus. *Adult. Mature. Young woman.* Here we go:

Dear Marlon,

What a satisfying revelation to find your correspondence in my mail receptacle today. I was immensely overjoyed to learn that you were my pursuer after all. Perhaps the miles and distance have

spoken to you in ways that no other circumstance could have ar-
ranged.

Now that's just corny. It's almost British; sounds like something I'd read in my English class. It's certainly not me. I tear this page out of the spiral, fold it several times, and throw it into the trash can as well. How can I tell Marlon that I want to be his friend—or more than his friend—without feeling goofy and embarrassed?

I'll have to get back to this later.

chapter thirteen

It's my last night of freedom, and I'm spending it with
Javon. He picks me up at 6:30 sharp, wearing all black
and looking so good I could just sop him up with a biscuit. I
just know my mom is gonna trip, but she doesn't. The whole
thing goes rather smoothly—he says hello, shakes my mom's
hand. She asks him what the plans are.

"Just dinner and a movie," is Javon's reply. He sounds like
he's rehearsed it.

All in all, I think my mom is impressed by him, though she
will probably never admit it, because then she would be saying
that I do have good judgment, after all.

I have to cherish this night, because who knows when we'll
be able to talk or see each other again. Javon and I have talked
about the big confession I have to make when I get home. He
says that I'm doing the right thing, even though it's not what
he would do.

"What would you do?" I ask him as he approaches a busy shopping center filled with restaurants and specialty shops.

He shrugs. "I don't know. I guess I'd try to come up on the money somehow."

"How? I mean, you can't just go out *looking* for money."

He serves up a smile with dimples on the side. "There are ways to find money."

"Like what?" I'm desperate.

He looks at me tentatively, then shakes his head. "You don't want to know."

I'm looking at Javon now for the first time in weeks, and he's cuter than I remember. If he were a little taller and didn't have those gold-rimmed teeth, he could be somebody's man in a music video, and I'd vote for him on *106 & Park* every time.

Javon takes me to Applebee's, and I've never been more excited to order a big, juicy bacon cheeseburger—hold the onions.

"You don't like onions?" Javon asks after the waiter leaves.

"I do, it's just . . ." If I could blush, I would. "I don't want to eat them tonight."

Javon rolls his lips between his teeth and watches me squirm beneath his glance. I swear he's beaming me with a hot laser. He teases, "You got big plans for tonight?"

I give him a smart-aleck laugh. "Ha, ha. Very funny."

"I've got big plans for us, too."

I'm looking at him when his eyes dart to my right and I hear a squeaky voice coming over my shoulder. "Is *this* the business you had to handle tonight?" I look to my right and see a very tall, slender, Christina Aguilera wannabee dressed in a red velvet jacket, a black leather skirt, and purple fishnets.

She's got long blond hair with black undertones, and it flows to her behind.

In a flash, Javon's expression goes from sexy to crazy as he tells this girl in so many words that she'd better shut up and leave. I move a little farther into the booth because I'm not particularly fond of mean girls standing over me. She looks me over and talks to Javon like she's got a bad taste in her mouth. "*This* your new woman?"

I answer for Javon. "Yes."

She grins and warns me, "He got you fooled."

Javon is fuming at this girl, and I'm getting concerned for her health. He stands up and gets in her face. "You betta bounce, Sheila. I ain't playin' with you."

"What are you going to do? Hit me again?" Sheila and Javon are frozen in a face-off. My eyes fall to his hands, and I see his fist clenching. Thank God Sheila takes a step back and turns away, slapping him with her fake hair. Javon watches her until she leaves the restaurant, and then he finally sits back down. For the next ten minutes he's trying to convince me that Sheila is a liar while he keeps one eye on his beloved car. This is crazy.

"Did you hit her?" I ask. This is, like, our whole relationship on the line.

He raises an eyebrow and pushes air out of his nose. "She hit me and I made her big Amazon-looking self raise up off of me. You see how aggressive she is, right?"

I agree with him, in a way. "Yeah?"

"I mean, you can't put your hands on somebody and expect not to get hit back, know what I'm sayin'?" he reasons.

I'm talking this thing out in my head and out loud at the same time. "But you've played football and stuff. You're stronger than she is. There's no way it could be a fair fight between the two of you."

"She should have thought about that before she hit me."

That little voice that spoke to me when I was at Derrick's house—the one that told me I shouldn't be there—is talking again. I have to shush this voice by thinking about all the good things Javon does: he makes me laugh, he makes me smile, he let me borrow his jacket when I was cold. Doesn't that count for something? He is also cute and fine and he has a job. No, he's not perfect, but who is? I know he's kinda rough and tough on the outside, but I see a big teddy bear on the inside. Isn't that what I'm supposed to do—look for the good things in people?

Besides, I'm not all loud and confrontational like Sheila. He might have hit her, but he wouldn't hit me. If he *did* try to hit me . . . well . . . I just wouldn't let that happen.

"Look, I wouldn't just come out and hit no girl for nothin'," Javon reemphasizes his point. "You understand what I'm sayin'?"

"Javon, I believe you, okay?" I'm not quite sure *why* I believe him, but I do.

"She's jealous because I never took *her* to Applebee's," Javon says as he blows out all of his anger and comes back to me.

I'm fishing for a compliment. "Why did you bring me and not her?"

"Because you're different. There's something about you, Karis. I don't know what it is, but you make me want to do the right thing."

Well, he obviously forgets about the right thing while we are at the movie theater. Behind me, there's a guy who keeps kicking my chair. Javon asks him twice to stop. When he does it a third time, Javon stands up and basically tells the guy that if he kicks my chair one more time, there will be a serious problem. I think the other guy is drunk, because he slurs his words together, "You sthinkin' yous somekinda soooperman?"

"I *got* your superman," Javon flares back.

Next thing you know, the man, his friend, Javon, and I are all being escorted out of the theater. Now Javon and I get a good look at the one who caused all the problems. He's probably sixty years old, maybe a hundred pounds. He looked way bigger in the theater—maybe because of the stadium seating. Once we get back in Javon's car, we laugh the whole thing off. The movie was stupid anyway.

We decide to go to Grand Prairie and look at the Christmas lights out by the lake. When I was younger, my dad used to take me to look at lights in some of the richest neighborhoods in Dallas. Riding through the exhibit with Javon feels like the good old days again, only instead of my daddy sitting next to me, I've got Javon sitting next to me—looking like a million bucks, I might add. Javon and I oooh and aaahh as though we have never experienced the magic of Christmas lights before. We stop and get hot chocolate to enjoy along the way.

"Look at those!" I exclaim just before Javon points my attention to another display. It is really turning out to be a special night for us, and I hope that next year we can do it again in *my* car.

It's getting close to eleven. Javon drives up to a convenience store so that we can get some gas and get me back home in time for my curfew. He hands me five dollars and asks me to go inside to pay. "Hey—I'm almost on E. You wanna put something with it?" he asks.

I look at him like he's crazy. The last thing I need to be

doing is giving away money. I've got exactly ten dollars in my pocket, and that's the last of my birthday loot. I walk into the store and pay the clerk. He says something to me in his thick Middle Eastern accent. I have no clue what he just said, but I don't want to be rude, so I smile and nod. Then I start looking around for gum or mints, because I am 99.9 percent sure that I will need very fresh breath in a minute.

When I get back out to the car, I walk to the passenger's side near Javon to get back into the car. That's when I see he's pumped to $8.98 already and counting.

He asks, "How much did you put with it?"

"I didn't put *anything* with it," I say.

He gives me the same look he gave Sheila earlier—a flash of anger and impatience. I'm confused about where this is coming from, and I am just about to ask him when he orders, "Go stand in front of the car."

"What?"

He says it with urgency. "Go stand in front of the car."

I don't know what this is all about, but I listen to him because . . . well . . . I don't know why.

I look back at the gas pump. He's up to $17.39 now, and I'm wondering what's going on. Just when I work up the nerve to ask him, he slams the gas pump handle back into its holder and yells at me, "Get in!"

I'm standing here like *what?* when he turns on the engine. "Get in the car!"

The store clerk is coming out of the store now, and I'm scared to death. I jump into Javon's car, and he burns rubber out of the parking lot. He's driving like a madman, swerving to the left and the right to bombard his way into traffic. Several people blow their horns at us.

"Hold on!" he orders.

"Javon!" I scream while clutching the dashboard for dear life. "What are you doing?"

He doesn't answer me until we get to my driveway. By this time, I have put the pieces of the puzzle together. He/we just stole some gas! I cannot believe this!

Javon puts the car in park, and I reach for the handle. "Karis, wait."

I lean back into my seat, though I'm not sure what kind of fool I must be to listen to him.

"I'm sorry, okay?"

"I thought you said I make you want to do the right thing!"

He throws his hands up in the air. "You do, it's just . . . sometimes I get this feeling . . . it's a rush . . . an adventure. And I do stuff that I know is bad, but if I can get away with it . . . I win."

I throw my hands into the air. "You think life is a big game, Javon? If the police had caught us, we would both be on our way to jail! Me with my stupid self—I'm the one on camera in the store, not you! And you had me at the front of your car to cover the license plate, right?"

Javon can't even look at me. He probably thought I wouldn't figure that one out. "Karis, I didn't plan for any of this to happen. I really thought you had put more money with my five dollars. I panicked when you said you hadn't because I don't have any more money on me. Honest."

"I have ten dollars, Javon. You could have asked me."

He shakes his head. "Naw. I ain't goin' out like that."

"You want to go to jail, though, and take me with you?" *Ooh, I am too through with him!* I grab the handle again, and

Javon locks the door from his side. "Let me out of here, Javon," I say.

"You gotta listen to me, Karis. I didn't mean for any of this to happen. Sheila, getting kicked out of the movies, the gas—none of it. This is . . . this is how my life goes. Since I left college, I've only had one bad thing happen after another. The only good thing I have in my life right now is you. Don't take that away from me, baby. I'm sorry, okay?"

I make the mistake of looking into his eyes, and I feel my resolve melting like butter on a hot frying pan. It's wonderful to know that I'm Javon's ray of hope. He's so handsome that he could have any girl he wants, but he's with *me*. He took *me* to Applebee's, he bought *me* popcorn at the movies, and *I'm* the last bit of hope he has left in the world. If I kick him to the curb, he might . . . I don't know . . . find somebody else, probably, and then he'll try to do all those nice things for her but she'll just be a gold digger and my baby will be hurt all over again. I can't let that happen to my boo.

He's gonna have to change, though.

"Javon, you've got to stop all these . . . adventures." I'm thinking. What would my mother say to encourage Javon right now? "You have to find some other way to get the rush. You didn't have all these problems when you were in school last year. Why are you having them now?"

"I had football then," he explains. His eyes light up when he talks about the sport. "I had dreams and goals and something to look forward to. Yeah, I had a lot of girls jockin' me, and I played them just like they played me. But on the real, football was my focus. Now I'm just another dude on the streets tryin' to make it."

I suggest, "Why don't you go back to school?"

"To me, the whole point of school is football. I don't wanna go back and be a nobody. Goin' to class every day, no fun, no competition. That's boring. I need some kind of excitement. Something new. I guess that's why I like you so much. You're different. You make me think."

"If you keep doing what you're doing, you're gonna end up in jail." Now I'm sounding like my mother all the way.

He looks at me point-blank and says, "Well, I can't let that happen, because then I'd lose you." Then he leans over to my side of the car and cups my chin in his hand. His whole face comes at mine, and I close my eyes as he kisses me in waves. I'm doing my best to kiss him back, but who am I kidding? I really don't know how to kiss. Javon does, though, and he finds me where I'm lost. I wish he wouldn't stop, yet at the same time I'm glad he does, because this whole thing is overwhelming: all these emotions—anger, fear, hurt, and then this make-you-slap-your-grandmomma kiss.

He smacks me on the lips one more time and says, "Let me walk you to the door."

We get out of the car and he kisses me again—this time on the cheek. We hold hands all the way to the door, and he finally says, "Well, I guess this is it for a while."

I almost forgot about what I have to do once I get inside my house. My stomach settles down, and a blanket of gloom covers me. "I guess so. I'll try to call you and text you when I can. You've got Tamisha's number in case something comes up, right?"

"Yeah. I'm gonna find me a job. Get my head together so next time we go out, it won't be so wild."

"That would be nice. Good night, Javon."

"Night, Karis."

chapter fourteen

My mom is waiting for me in the living room, and I haven't even closed the door before she starts with the questions. Where did we go? What happened? Did I conduct myself like a young lady? Was he a gentleman?

"We had a nice time, Momma," I say, thinking only of the Christmas lights and the last five minutes of the date, which, by the way, made up for everything else as far as I'm concerned.

I'm not saying another word, because I know that anything I say can and will be used against me one day in the court of Janice Reed.

My mom stands and tightens her robe around her waist. I realize now that she doesn't really want to know what happened on my date. She only wanted to make sure I made it in safely *before* eleven o'clock. As I watch her walk away, I see her yawn on the way to her bedroom, and I decide that now is the best time to tell her about the phone bill situation. She's tired, and she may not have the energy to really lay into me. "Mom, I need to talk to you."

She stops cold, grabs the collar of her robe, and faces me with this look of horror in her eyes. She's thinking this has something to do with Javon—probably something to do with sex. Maybe it will come as a relief that I'm only asking her to help with a phone bill, not a grandchild.

"Momma, something happened with Sydney."

She sighs in relief for herself and takes another deep breath for the Normans. "Is she okay?"

"Yeah, she's fine." Again, my mother exhales. I can't let her get too ungrateful, so I bust out with it. "Last month, I used Angelique's phone and the phone bill is like nine hundred dollars. I was hoping I could try to help her with half of it because it is kinda my fault."

The hands come from her collar to her hips now. "Karis, why were you using Angelique's phone?"

"'Cause I couldn't use my phone."

"Oh, now I see." She taps her chin with a forefinger as her mind races to fill in the blanks that I tried to leave open. "So when I grounded you, you and Miss Sydney decided to disregard your punishment. Now y'all done ran up a thousand-dollar bill and you expect *me* to pay for it?"

"It's nine hun—"

"Might as well be a thousand! Might as well be a *million*, 'cause I ain't got it either way!" my mother roars as her eyes fill with rage. I underestimated the amount of energy she had left tonight. She has been revived with anger. "Do you think I'm made of money? You think I can just write a check for every mistake you make?"

I know the answer to both of those questions is no, but the word is caught in my throat. My mother rushes toward me, snatches my shirt, and pulls me so close our eyeballs are almost touching. "Answer me, Karis!"

"N-no, ma'am." I'm afraid to breathe right now.

"And you know I just sacrificed three weeks' worth of overtime opportunities so I could take you to driver's education! I don't have *any* extra money right now!" My mother releases her grip on my shirt, throws her hands in the air, and screams, "Jesus! Lord, Jesus, help me!"

She goes into her bedroom and pulls out her phone book while I'm standing in the hallway wondering if I should go to my room, wait here, or run away. She picks up the phone, and I'm waiting to hear who she's calling. It's Sydney's mom. They're talking about us as though I'm not standing there. I can tell from her tone that my mom and Mrs. Norman are on the same page. They're both mad at me and Sydney, and they both think we need to split the bill because we are both at fault.

"Well, let me call her father, Debra," my mom says. "I'll give you a call tomorrow. All right. You, too."

I'm still standing in the hallway, and my heart is all the way down at my feet. If she calls my dad, my car will be over. I step into her bedroom as she's preparing to dial his number. "Momma, can I talk to you? Pleeeease?"

She looks back at me over her shoulder with one finger on one of the phone's buttons. I cannot let her dial that number. "Momma, I'll get a job or something. Anything to help them pay the bill."

"We're going to have to *reimburse* them for the bill, Karis. They've already paid it. We're playing catch-up right now, you understand? We *owe* them. We ain't got time to wait for you to find a job!" My momma can't stand owing money. I've heard her say that on many occasions.

"What I don't understand is what took you so long to tell me." She turns off the phone, and I feel some relief.

"I wanted to tell you, but—"

"But you couldn't tell me until *after* you did what you wanted to do tonight, huh?"

God, please tell me how my mother figures all these things out so quickly!

"Debra said Sydney's been crying her eyes out over this bill, and I haven't seen you shed one tear! What's wrong with you, Karis? You don't care about anyone but yourself! You are your father's daughter . . . just selfish! Don't think about nobody but you!"

I wish she would have punched me in my stomach instead of saying that. Tears spill out of my eyes and my mom turns her back to me, shaking her head and dialing my dad's number. I go to my room and collapse on my bed. How can my mom say those mean things to me? If I only cared about myself, I wouldn't have told her about the bill knowing that I was going to get in trouble. If I was so selfish, I wouldn't serve in the education ministry by tutoring every summer. I am not selfish! Why can't she give me credit for the things I do right?

I can hear her talking to my dad now. A few minutes later, my mother opens my bedroom door. "Your daddy wants to talk to you." She brings the phone to me, and I wait for her to leave the room.

"Hello?"

"Baby girl, you messed up this time."

My voice cracks. "I know, Daddy. I'm sorry."

"Shhh, don't cry," he calms me. I wish he were here so I could curl up into a little ball and cry on his shoulder. "I've gotta take some of the money I was gonna use for your car and pay Sydney's parents, you know? I don't have an extra four-hundred-something dollars sitting around."

I'm crying my eyes out now, and snot is flying out of my nose. I have waited sixteen years for this car, and now two thousand minutes of peak time is standing in the way! "But Daddy, I can get a job and drive myself to work and earn enough money to pay them back in a couple of months."

"They need their money now, just like everybody else. Bills wait for no one."

"Well," I try again, "can I get a different car? One that's four hundred dollars less than the other ones?"

"Karis, you disobeyed." His voice is firm. I can't stand it when my daddy gets mad at me. "You don't get to make deals when you break the rules."

Reality hits. There's no way I am getting my car for Christmas. "When can I get another chance?"

"Probably not until I get my next bonus at the end of March."

The end of March! That's after spring break! I whimper a little longer, and I can almost hear my father wincing. "Put your momma back on the phone," he says.

I expect my mom to come back in the room and fuss at me some more, but she doesn't. Her silence is worse than getting yelled at because at least I know what she's thinking when she's yelling. She hasn't come in to repossess any of my communication tools. I'm wondering, *Is this the end?* I know kids who do everything short of committing murder and their parents don't do anything about it. I've always envied those kids, but not tonight. If my mom doesn't try to do something to me, then maybe she has given up on me.

After about half an hour, I decide it's safe to go to the restroom. I look under her door. I see the dim, yellow light of her lamp and hear a steady, familiar rhythm of words. She's praying.

When I finish in the bathroom, her lamp is off and I'm pretty sure she's in bed. I go back to my room and decide that it would be a good idea to tell God my side of the story. I tell Him about everything from Sydney to Javon to my mother telling me that I'm selfish just like my daddy. "I know I messed up, God, and I'm sorry. Please help me to stop getting in trouble." I almost forget to pray for Marlon, but he pops into my mind at the last minute, so I recite my prayer for him again.

The only good thing I can think of in all of this is that school is out for the holidays. Then again, that could be a bad thing. When I'm grounded, school is my only form of socialization. This time, I'm not gonna try to work around it. I did the crime, I'll do the time; get it over with.

Dear Me:

I might as well be a total nun who has taken a vow of silence and misery. Everything in my life is jacked up—except for Javon and Marlon (if I ever figure out what to say to him). And my grades. My mom, my dad, my friends, everything else is crazy. I don't even know what to write to Marlon.

I just want to live a normal life, you know? Go to school, do my homework, go to church, have some friends, have a boyfriend, and get along with my parents. Is that too much to ask? I'd also like a CAR, but that is totally out of the picture.

                    Karis Abnormal-and-Traveling-by-Foot Reed

chapter fifteen

Since it's the Christmas season, my mom is really busy working overtime at the hospital. She also has several speaking engagements. All of this means that I'll be spending more time with my father. On the way to his house, my mom is fussing at me. "Karis, your father and I have been talking." I don't even ask what they have been discussing, because right now, I really don't care. It's been four days since I got to talk to my baby, Javon, for more than fifteen minutes, so my attitude is bad.

She keeps talking. "What do you think about spending more time at your father's house?"

"Two weekends a month?" I ask.

"No," she explains. "Something more permanent."

I'm stunned! "You mean *living* with him?"

"Well." My mother shakes her head, keeping her eyes fixed

on the road ahead. "Clearly, I'm having a hard time raising you. You're . . . trying to stress your independence. I'm trying to make sure you don't make choices that could bring serious consequences. We keep butting heads. I don't know, Karis, maybe your father can do a better job."

It makes me sad that my mom doesn't think she's a good mom, because she *is*—but this is *my* life. If she would just let me live it, we could get along fine. The only problem with this picture, of course, is that she calls the shots because she's providing me with a place to stay, food, and clothes. Plus, she's my mother, which trumps everything. *Oooh, this is so frustrating!*

Shereese's car isn't here, which explains why my mom is going into my dad's house. I grab my bag from the backseat, and we walk to the door. My daddy greets us with hugs—a real one for me, a fake one for my mom. They both claim the reason they divorced is that they were on two different paths in life. My dad says my mom is married to her careers. My mom says my dad wants to relive his youth. If you ask me, they're both right and wrong at the same time.

My mom sits at the dining room table, and my dad does, too. It takes me a moment to realize I am at an intervention. *My* intervention. "Karis, sit down," Daddy orders. My mom must have put him up to this, because sitting down and talking is not his style. My behind is barely in the seat and already I'm feeling warm. "Your mother and I have been talking about making a few changes. What do you think of moving in with me?"

"You and Shereese?"

My mom breathes in deeply, and I can almost see smoke coming from her ears.

"No. Just me."

It's funny. I really thought I'd be excited to move in with my dad. But I'm not, because basically they're telling me that I'm such a bad person that my own mother is kicking me out.

I turn to my mom. "Do *you* want me to move in with Dad?"

She can't speak. She just shakes her head no. I feel a big lump coming up in my throat. My mom is making this all dramatic. She wipes a tear from her eye. "It's hard being a single parent, Karis. I've been doing this for five years now, and I could use . . . a break."

My dad cannot stand to see my mom cry. He'd rather see her scream and yell than cry, so he cuts the intervention short. "Well, we don't have to decide anything tonight. Let's just give it some time."

My mom kisses me on the cheek as she walks out the door, and I'm completely torn. My dad follows her outside, and they keep talking on the porch. I sneak into my dad's bathroom so I can hear the discussion through the window. I know it's wrong to dip in their conversation, but they're talking about *my* life. Don't I have a right to know what's going to happen to me?

They're talking about child support. My dad says that she should count the money he's repaying the Normans as this month's child support. My mom says that's not right because this is an unexpected expense. They're going back and forth about the money, and I wish they would get back to the discussion about me. Things are getting pretty heated, just like old times. They're arguing about the "car fund" and whether or not my daddy ever had the money for my car in the first place. Dad says he did.

"You're lying!" from my mom.

"See, you always jumping to conclusions, Janice!" from my dad.

I cover my ears and look toward the sky. These two are hopeless. Why can't they just talk things out like regular parents?

My mom leaves before somebody calls the police on them, thank goodness. The first thing my dad does when he comes back inside is call Shereese and invite her over for dinner. I look forward to seeing Shereese again. Who knows? Maybe we could become great friends. She could be the older sister I never had.

"Daddy, can we order pizza?"

He mumbles yeah as he rubs a hand through his head, calming himself. His hands are big and rough. Usually, my dad is on top of his game, but right now, he could use some lotion.

"You plan on bustin' that ash sometime soon?" I ask him, trying to get him back to his normal self.

"Bust *what*?" He stiffens and looks at me with a scowl on his face.

"Bust that *ashy* skin on your hands," I say a little louder.

My dad's facial features slip back into their normal slots. "For a minute there, I thought you were cussin' now."

I roll my eyes playfully and smack my lips. "Daddy, please. I'm not *that* bad."

He crosses his arms and leans back on the kitchen counter. "But you do think you're bad, huh? To some extent?"

I mimic his gesture, leaning back against the microwave. "No. I might be a little bad, but I'm not real, real bad like some kids I know. I mean, I love you guys and I go to church and I pray, so I can't be *that* bad, I don't think."

"Well, why are you giving your mother such a hard time?"

"I'm not . . . I just . . . stuff keeps *happenin'* to me. I don't *plan* for all these problems to come in my life. They just *do*." I try to animate my analogy by putting my hands out in front of me, parallel, and moving them in a straight line. "It's like, I'm trying to walk this straight line and mind my own business and then—BAM—trouble gets in my way." My hands go flying everywhere to symbolize the random chaos that comes into my life. I know it probably sounds and looks like a sorry explanation, but it's the truth.

"So, the skipping half a day of school last semester just *happened*?" He raises an eyebrow and waits for the explanation I can't exactly give him without giving too much information.

I did have a perfectly good reason for skipping. Tamisha had cramps, and Mr. Littley was not about to let her sit out or go to the nurse—partly because she'd faked cramps the week before. Anyway, *somebody* had to go with her to Walgreens to get some Midol because she was doubled over in pain. Once we were off campus, there was no way we could get back on without getting caught, so we just went back to her house and chilled for the rest of the day. "It was a female medical emergency," I say to my father.

He brings up another incident. "And the zero plus detention that you got in skills for living? How do you get *a zero* in a *cooking* class?"

I'm not going out like this! "Daddy, I worked really hard the rest of the six weeks to make up that zero. I can't have my GPA going down over a cheesecake."

"That still doesn't answer my question," he corners me.

"Okay, I can explain. What had happened was, it was me,

this girl named Allissa, and this *crazy* boy—called Booyah—in my group. I mean for real, Daddy, he is crazy.

"We had made a cheesecake. Allissa was standing next to the oven getting ready to put the cake in. I was standing next to Allissa, and Booyah was standing next to me—right next to our sink. Booyah was acting all crazy, trying to splash water on me. So when I jumped back, I bumped into Allissa and Allissa dropped the whole cheesecake into the oven." My father looks at me with an unbelieving smirk. "I swear, Daddy, if she hadn't dropped that cake so she could use her hands to catch herself on the countertop, her whole face would have been in the oven.

"So then, Miss Rossenburg comes over and starts hollering at all three of us, telling us we gotta pay for those ingredients because she doesn't have money in her budget and blah-zay this, blah-zay that. Me and Allissa were like, 'We ain't payin' for nothin' because it was Booyah's fault,' but the teacher wasn't tryin' to hear us. So all three of us got a zero, plus me and Allissa got detention because Miss Rossenburg said we were disrespectful or whatever.

"Now, is that fair, Daddy?"

I take it that he doesn't want to discuss this issue anymore, because a smirk comes across his face. He uncrosses his arms, turns his back to me, and picks up the phone to order the pizza.

Why can't adults just admit when they're wrong?

chapter sixteen

Shereese and the pizza arrive at the same time. My dad pays for our food and lets Shereese in. I'm sitting in the living room watching television when I see my dad walk by with pizza and Shereese following him into the kitchen. She barely speaks to me, and her face has "stank mood" written all over it.

This is my dad's second argument in an hour. Their voices are muffled, but I can just make out my mom's name and something about the deed to this house. I need more information. Is my dad moving? If he's moving, that means I might have to switch schools! No way am I leaving Central! I turn down the television and take a few steps toward the hallway so I can get a better understanding of the situation.

"Shereese, I did not kick you out," my dad is pleading.

"And I am not letting my ex-wife dictate what happens between you and me."

She counters, "Wake up, Reginald! You think it's a coincidence that just when I move in, your daughter starts acting a fool and your ex-wife comes up with the bright idea to have her come live with you?"

Hey! That's not true! If I had thought of the plan, it would have been great, actually, but she's giving me too much credit here. I had no idea Shereese was living with my daddy when I borrowed Angelique's phone.

Shereese walks to my dad's room. I nearly break my neck trying to scramble back to the couch before I'm discovered eavesdropping. Then she travels from my dad's room to the third bedroom and slams the door behind herself.

Shereese's temper tantrum leaves my daddy and me watching movies together, which is perfectly fine. If she wants to act all childish, like this is a competition, she needs to recognize that she will never beat me. I am a daddy's girl, and that's all there is to it.

My dad conks out after the second movie. I don't suppose he's going back to his bedroom tonight, so I cover him with a blanket. I turn off the DVD and turn the channel to ESPN because my daddy likes to sleep with the television on.

When I make it back to my room, I close the door behind me and start getting undressed. Okay, Shereese has obviously not lived in this house long enough to know that the wall between my room and the third bedroom is paper thin. Or maybe she thinks I'm still in the living room. Either way, I can hear every word coming out of her mouth as she talks on the phone. I'm really trying not to listen to her . . . she's just so . . . loud. In the past, she's always acted like this proper, quiet person. I didn't know she had it in her. Now, she sounds like Tamisha or something.

"I really don't care what his ex-wife thinks! She can kiss me where the sun don't shine . . . I know . . . Mmm-hmm . . . that's exactly what I say. If she can't keep the girl under control, what makes him think *he* can? He ain't nothin' but a big pushover. . . . How he gon' kick me out so his daughter can move in? . . . Oh, no, he don't *want* me to get involved with his daughter, 'cause I'll jack her up one good time and . . . ha! Ha! I know, girl!"

My bottom lip is on the floor! I know she is *not* talking about *me*!

"Girl, I don't know. I think she was on somebody's cell phone. Who knows? Mmm-hmm . . . his ex ain't *too* holy—she got pregnant at sixteen . . . how she gon' judge me and Reginald? . . . She ain't too good a minister *now* with her daughter runnin' around like a straight-up hot-momma on the streets. Spent the night over some boy's house a few months ago . . . yeah, right, huh? The apple don't fall far from the tree . . . Ha! Ha! All I know is—*I'm* the woman of *this* house, and if I have to lay down some new rules, I will. And if Reginald has a problem with it, he can leave, too, 'cause by the time I finish with him, *I'll* get this house, okay?"

Aw, naw. It ain't goin' down like this. I've got to go wake up my daddy. I've got to knock Shereese out. My heart is pounding in my chest about as loud as I'm pounding on the third bedroom door. Shereese opens, with the phone to her chest. She says in a sweet, soft tone, "Yes?"

My mouth is open and I hardly know where to start. As mad as I am, I could just let my fists do the talking. For Shereese's sake, it's a good thing the words finally come to me. "Do you have a problem with me or my momma, because if you do, you need to let us know."

"No. What *you* need to do is stay out of grown folks' business," Shereese snaps back, bugging her eyes out at me.

Oh, it's *on* and *poppin'* now! I take a step closer and get into as much of her personal space as the door between us will allow. I'm trying to keep my voice under control, but it's getting louder with each word. "If you're talking about me and my momma, it *is* my business. You ain't all grown, either. What you doin' with an old man like my daddy anyway?"

"That, too, is none of your business."

I guess my yelling woke up my daddy, because here he comes down the hall. Now that he's standing right next to us, Shereese clicks off the phone and steps out into the hallway all big and bad. I don't want her to get in the first word, so I blurt out, "Daddy, Shereese was on the phone talking about—"

"Why were you listening to her phone conversation?" he says, cutting me off.

"I wasn't trying to. She was—"

"Karis, you have an excuse for everything, you know that?" He pushes my testimony aside. The same smirk he had earlier is back.

Now my heart stops its heavy pounding. I wonder if it's beating at all. My dad looks at Shereese, looks at me, and then looks back at his girlfriend. I have seen people do this on game shows, like they are trying to pick which door to open. I'm wondering why this is even a choice. I have lied to a lot of people, but I don't lie to my dad because . . . well, I guess because he doesn't really have any rules to break. So why would I start lying to him now?

Shereese senses my father's hesitation and jumps right in

to smooth things over her own way, putting one hand on my father's chest. "Honey, I was talking to Jasmine on the phone. Blowing off steam."

"Ooh, Daddy! No she wasn't!"

My father massages his temples. "Let's all go to bed, okay? We can deal with this tomorrow."

Shereese rolls her neck to one side and tells my father, "There's nothing to deal with. I don't debate with children."

My dad shakes his head and repeats, "Let's go to bed." Shereese follows him down the hallway to the master bedroom. My dad closes the door behind her. He doesn't even look at me again.

I cannot believe my dad just punked out like that! How he just gon' listen to Shereese over me? And why did he let Shereese talk to him like that—"I don't argue with children." I'm not *children*—I'm Reginald's young adult daughter! She betta ask somebody!

I should have popped her. If I could play it again, I would steal her in the jaw, and then she would hit me back, and we would fight, and then I'd call the police because I'm a minor, and she would go to jail, and my momma would come pick me up right now.

I go straight to the third bedroom, which is the only one on the hall with a phone. My first instinct is to call my momma, but I don't know how I'm going to explain all this to her. Besides, she's at work, and I know that before it's all over with she'd come pick me up, and I'd be in trouble for calling her at work and making her miss time-and-a-half pay.

My next best bet is Javon. I don't care if my dad catches me on the phone. If my dad comes into this room and catches me on the phone, that will just be too bad!

When Javon answers his phone, my emotions spill out of me. I'm crying and I can't stop.

"Karis, what's wrong?"

"Mydaddygirflriendisstupidhelistenstoher."

"What?"

I sniff a few times and catch my breath. "My daddy's girlfriend is stupid and he listens to her."

"I thought you said she was cool."

I squeeze my eyes shut tight again and ride out another wave of grief. "I was wrong."

"What happened?"

Javon's calmness eventually reaches me through the phone. He listens as I tell him everything that happened. I do my best to tell him word-for-word.

"That's messed up," he says when I'm finished. "What are you gonna do?"

"I don't know. What *can* I do?"

He hums as he thinks. "You want me to steal her car?"

Now I'm laughing like crazy. I'm trying to be all serious and stuff and Javon makes this wild offer. "No, I do not want you to steal her car."

He laughs now. "Hey, I'm just tryin' to keep a smile on my girl's face."

Javon is right. I am smiling, thanks to him. "Thank you, Boo."

"For what?"

"For just being here."

"Anything for you." He hugs me with his words.

We talk some more about his new job at a car detailing place. He starts tomorrow. Javon loves cars, so this should be a job that he enjoys even though the pay isn't so great. I hope he can stay there until something better comes along. I remind him, "Okay, Javon, no stealing."

"No stealing."

"No *embezzling*."

"No embezzling," he agrees. "There's nothing there to embezzle. People bring their cars in; they pick 'em up. No money passes through my hands except maybe a tip."

We decide that as soon as I get off punishment and he gets a paycheck, we're going out again. "Whatchu wanna do this time?" he asks.

"Not run into any of your old exes, not get kicked out of a movie, not steal gasoline," I say.

"Well, there's only one thing we can do—especially if you don't want to run into any of my ex-girlfriends," he says with a little too much pride.

"What's that?"

"Go someplace nice and quiet. Just me and you."

Roller-coaster tickle.

"Someplace like where?"

"I don't know. Somebody's house . . . someplace where we can be alone. You down?"

Big *fat* roller-coaster tickle. I do want to be alone with Javon, but I'm not sure about going to somebody's house. "I don't know."

"Whatchu sayin'?"

I'm trying to explain myself without sounding as though I don't like him. "I want to be alone, too . . . it's just . . . I don't want anything . . . to . . . happen . . . that might . . . change things."

He hums again. Thinking. "Karis, have you been with a guy before?"

"Not . . . like . . . all alone, except for this one time, but he was really just a friend."

"Straight?"

"Yeah. Why would I lie about that?"

"Dang. I didn't know there were any good girls left." I can hear the smile in his voice. I'm still undecided about whether this smile is a good thing or not. "When you told me that you were in trouble for being at a boy's house, I just assumed you were with guys all the time."

I can't believe he said that! I smack real loud so he can hear me. "So all this time you've been thinking I'm some kind of hoochie!"

"No! I didn't say that. I'm just sayin' . . ." His voice trails off. Then he asks, "So, do you like the way things are right now between us, or do you think maybe we should try to make this relationship a little more serious?"

Isn't it serious already?

When I don't answer, Javon calms me by saying, "We'll just take things slow, okay? I'm gettin' to know you and I like you, so . . . I'm sayin' . . . let's just go out and see what happens from there." Here's what he means: *Karis, I am not going to pressure you into anything. I almost love you because you, Karis, are different and special.*

And, really, isn't this the kind of guy my mom always says I should be with? The kind who respects me and respects my decisions? I've found him! I am going to be Mrs. Javon Montriece Dawson!

My dad takes me home in the morning. We're silent the whole trip. I don't have anything to say to him, and I'm praying that he will not say anything to me about stupid Shereese. When I get home, he tries to help me with my bags. I carry them myself, use my key to open the door, and barely say good-bye to him before the door starts to shut in his face.

He puts out a hand to stop it from closing. "Karis, about last night."

I rest all of my weight on my right side, puff out my lips, and wait to hear exactly what he has to say about last night—not that it matters.

"Shereese was upset. It was late. I was tired, and so were you."

Speak for yourself. I wasn't tired. I shift my weight to the left, letting my body do the talking for me. If I open my mouth to speak, my tough mask will disintegrate.

"Let it go, okay?"

He's looking at me now with a give-me-a-break expression. *Does everyone need a break from me these days?* His eyes catch the twinkle from the Christmas tree lights. I remember when I used to think my daddy was the next best thing to Santa Claus. Now he's a big Grinch! I gotta stop looking at him before I start crying again.

I look down at the floor and tell my father good-bye. I don't want him to see me cry. He might go back and tell Shereese some more of my business.

He steps back inside the house and hugs me. "I love you. You know that, right?"

There goes the mask. I'm crying into his shirt, wondering how he could hurt me and still love me. "Yes."

"Nothing and no one will ever change how much I love you." He squeezes me one more time before he leaves.

I clear my face of all the tears before I go to my mom's

room. She's asleep on top of her comforter, still wearing her nursing uniform, all the way down to her shoes. She must have sat down on the edge of the bed, lain back, then fallen asleep immediately. Quietly, I walk around the bed and re-move the shoes from her feet. She lets out a loud snore, and I decide to let the situation with Shereese rest. My mom needs her sleep.

chapter seventeen

Our church is having its annual mother-daughter Christmas dinner. The last couple of years, my mom was the speaker. They decided to give her a rest this year. In a way, I'm glad. When my mom has a new speech, she practices for days, sometimes weeks, ahead of time. She records herself, and I have to listen to her CDs over and over again in the car, so by the time I hear her speak at the event, it is completely boring to me.

Today is different. We're here like regular people, enjoying the dinner and having a good time with each other. I was a little afraid about how things would go between us, given all the drama that has gone down over the past few months. My mom hasn't really spoken to me too much since we had that conversation about me moving out—partly because she's been working like crazy to make enough money to cover my behind with Sydney. Even though Sydney still isn't talking to me, I know it was the right thing to do. I'm vowing to myself to pay my mom back this money. As soon as I get a job, I'll start saving like twenty dollars a week. Next Christmas I'll present her with an envelope full of cash money to make up for all the mess I put her through this year. Well, maybe I'll have to start saving in the summer, because there's prom and all this spring. No matter what, I'm giving her at least four hundred and fifty dollars for Christmas next year.

I can tell that she's making a serious effort to put the drama out of her mind and let tonight be what it's supposed to be—a celebration of Jesus' birth. She popped in her favorite Christmas CD and sang along all the way to church. Now we sit next to each other, surrounded by other mothers with their teenage daughters. These other moms look *old* than a *mug*. They must be at least forty. Some of them even have gray hair. My mom and I are both wearing boot-cut jeans and stretchy shirts. I hate to admit it, but we look good together. Before my mom started ministering to other young ladies, people at church used to do a double take when she told them she was my mother. It didn't take long for them to figure out that she must have been very young when she had me.

Once, when I was in elementary school, my teacher thought my mom was my big sister. She refused to have a conference until my mom showed her a license. Then the teacher said real soft, "Babies havin' babies." My mom got up and left the classroom in tears.

At first, my mom was ashamed of being a teenage parent. Even though she later married my father, there was always someone looking down on her. But then one day I guess she got tired of it and decided that instead of hiding behind her past, she would tell her story and give God credit for turning the situation around. My mom went back to school and got her degree. Now she's a registered nurse and a motivational speaker. I don't tell my mom, but I am proud of her. And nights like tonight, when we're both made up and dressed up, I look at her and think to myself, *Yes! I'll still be cute when I'm thirty-two!*

The young men's choir sings a few Christmas carols. I see Henry among them. He's improving in the body category. I might have to put him back in my cell phone. On second thought, maybe not. I'm cutting back on guys. The other week, that guy I met at the Gap called. I considered him for a moment; then he got all goofy and started talking about video games. Had to let that brother go. If things keep going well between me and Javon, I might have to let all these other brothers go except Marlon. Marlon is for the future, Javon is for now.

There is so much talking and singing that my mother and I really don't get to say a lot to each other throughout the program. On the way back home, she starts off the conversation by teasing me. "I saw you lookin' at handsome Henry."

"I was not." I lie like a rug, and she knows it.

My mother smiles and dismisses my words. "Yeah, right."

I turn the tables. "You sure kept lookin' at that man on the organ, too."

She sucks in air and tries to deny it.

"Yeah, right," I tease her.

She laughs, then slides into, "Oh, Karis, I wish we could have more talks like this. Seems like the only time we talk is when I'm yelling at you or you're making an excuse." I'm trying to read her face and see if she's still joking or not. Can't tell, so I shut my mouth and start watching the streetlights go by.

"Hello? You still here?"

"Yes."

She pushes me. "Any response?"

"I . . . think it would be nice, too, if we didn't have so much yelling."

"What about the excuses?"

This is a trick question. One false move and this could go bad real quick. "I wish I could stop making up excuses, too."

"That makes no sense to me." My mom looks me in the eye with a gentle expression and asks, "What do you mean?"

I try my best to explain it to her the way I explained it to my dad. Things happen, and one thing leads to another, and before I know it, I have to make up an excuse to keep from getting in trouble.

"You know that excuses are often lies, right?"

"Yes, ma'am."

My mom takes a deep breath and keeps her temper in check. "I'm going to tell you the same thing I'd tell a young lady in my ministry at church. If you want to stop telling lies and making excuses, start walking in integrity. Say what you mean, mean what you say, and always tell the truth."

"Yeah, but what if I do something that's gonna make you mad?" I question.

"Well, when you walk in integrity, you make decisions and take actions based on what's right," she explains. "The truth comes easier after that."

"But what if I do what I *think* is the right thing to do and I *still* make you mad?"

"If you try to do the right thing but it turns out to be the wrong thing, I'm not going to get mad at you. I can't get mad at you for not knowing the future." My mom glances at me again. "Look, Karis, nobody's perfect. Everybody messes up. Sometimes we mess up because we don't know any better. Sometimes we mess up because we didn't think things through. Sometimes we have the best intentions but things just fall apart. What separates a person with integrity from everyone else is this: a person with integrity tells the truth—most importantly, to herself. I want you to think about that."

This is too deep for me. I can accept the "do the right thing" part, but I already know that if I start telling the truth, I'll get into even more trouble and my life will be even more miserable. I start looking out the window again. I'm surprised my mom isn't trying to pound this integrity thing into me right now. She slides her Fred Hammond CD into the player and we listen to music the rest of the way home.

My mom is off to the store today to do some last-minute shopping, which gives me about an hour of phone time. I feel a little bad about sneaking to get on the phone, especially since that big "integrity" talk. I'll make these calls quickly.

I call Tamisha first. She fills me in on all the latest gossip: Rene Karowsky is pregnant; Mercedes Gordon and Amy Hill had a car accident, but they're okay; Sydney's coach says that Sydney can still go to summer camp on some kind of scholarship, maybe. The mention of Sydney's name sends a pang of guilt through me. Tamisha picks up on my silence and asks, "Are you there?"

"Yes, I'm here." I have to know. "Tamisha, is Sydney still mad at me?"

Tamisha admits, "Yep."

"Why? I mean, we *gave* her the money."

I get the feeling that Tamisha is trying to make things sound better than they are. "She's upset because it took you a while to talk to your mom about it. I mean for real, Karis, you tripped at first."

"I didn't trip—I freaked! We both freaked at first."

Tamisha assumes the role of mediator and volunteers to call Sydney on my behalf. "I'll tell her that you're really sorry and that you beg her forgiveness."

"I didn't say all that."

"Well, you'd better say something close to it if you want her friendship again," Tamisha fusses. "The way Sydney sees it, you almost cost her a career in basketball. And did you say something about her always hanging around with girls and not liking boys?"

I remember it, vaguely. "I was just saying something because she said something about Javon. Whatever I said in retaliation, I'm sure I didn't mean it. You think I should call her?"

"No. Let me go in with the white flag first. I'll let you know when it's safe to call her."

"Well, don't rush. I'm grounded again."

Tamisha laughs. "What else is new? Bye, Karis."

I hang up with Tamisha, thinking about her last remarks. Why is it that I'm the only one who's grounded all the time? Tamisha isn't an angel. She's done her fair share of sneaking around—she even let a guy drive her car one time! And Sydney writes vocabulary definitions on her hand when she gets ready to take a test she hasn't studied for. I don't know. Maybe I've got too much free time on my hands. Maybe if I had a job or played a sport, I wouldn't have time to get in trouble. No, then my grades probably wouldn't be so good. Out of Tamisha, Sydney, and me, I'm ranked the highest in our class. You can't win them all! So why am I always the one getting caught doing stupid stuff? Other people do all kinds of things that never come to light. There are people who've committed felonies who have more freedom than I do right now! *Huuuh!* I can't think about this too long or I'll get depressed.

It's time to call Javon. He's probably at work. Maybe I can at least leave him a message. "Hi, Javon, it's Karis. I miss you! I know you're working hard. Keep it up! I wanted to get you something for Christmas, but you know the cash situation around here. Anyway, just wanted you to know that I'm thinking about you. I'll call you when I get another chance. Bye!" I kiss him through the phone and hang up. Then I call back one more time just so I can hear his voice again on recording. I miss Javon so much!

I've only got one more time to see my dad before Christmas. Even though he had to pay that phone bill, he still bought gifts for me. I, of course, have zero dollars, so my mom bought his gift on my behalf. Today, two days before Christmas, he and I will spend some time together and open our gifts. The first year my parents were divorced, I liked the idea of having two Christmases. Now, it just feels like two half-Christmases.

Shereese's car is in the driveway, so my mom drops me off and makes sure I'm inside before leaving. I give my father a big hug at the doorway, and he's acting suspicious already. He pulls me aside before we even get past the dining room.

"Karis, remember what I said. Don't start none, won't be none, okay?"

I'm not going to let Shereese run all over me, if that's what he's asking. "I can let it go if *she* lets it go."

I promise, it is the most wack pre-Christmas gift exchange ever. Jesus would be ashamed to be at His own birthday party. Shereese sits on the love seat with her arms folded, rocking her foot back and forth. My dad tries to get her in the spirit of things. "Look, Shereese, Karis got me one of those electronic organizers."

"Hmph. I guess I'll have to take back the one I bought and get you something else."

My dad got me an iTunes gift card, some Bath and Body Works stuff, and a J-Lo warm-up suit. The pants look a little long, so I stand up and hold them against my body.

My dad tries again to get Shereese to act right. "You think they're too big for her, honey?"

She turns up her full lips until the pink interior shows. "No. They look fine to me."

I've had enough of her, and so has my dad. He asks Shereese to come with him to the bedroom so they can talk. They go in there for a few minutes, there's some yelling, and next thing I know Shereese busts out of their room crying. This girl is a drama queen for real! "I loved you, Reginald! Remember that!"

And she storms out of the house with my dad chasing her. "I love you, too, Shereese. We can work this out, baby. Don't leave."

Good riddance!

My dad comes back in the living room and throws away the wrapping paper that's all over the floor.

"What's wrong with her, Daddy?"

He shakes his head. "This is really tough on Shereese. She says she's not used to being number two."

Glad to know I'm still number one in his life.

"I keep trying to tell her that she's not number two, you know? You're *both* number one."

"It's a *tie* between me and her?" That ain't right.

My father explains, "It's not a *tie*. These are two different spaces in my life. One is for a daughter, the other is for a companion. You understand what I'm saying?"

I guess I get it. I have a place in my heart for my dad and a different place in my heart for Javon. Marlon is, like, in my lung—which is still a vital organ, mind you. It's weird how all three of them are so high up on the ladder of my life.

This night, I decide to go ahead and start reading the novel I've selected for my literary analysis essay, which I'll be doing next semester. I picked a book called *Things Fall Apart* by this African guy named Chinua Achebe. Mrs. Clawson says it's a classic, which almost made me change my mind. So far, it seems okay. They just keep having these big huge celebrations for like every single thing that happens in the village! Somebody gets lost, there's a feast. Somebody decides to go looking for the lost person, there's a feast. They both come back, there's a feast.

I wonder if we'll have a feast when Marlon comes home. Thinking of Marlon, I open my spiral and try once again to write him a letter.

Dear Marlon,
I'm scared. Actually, I'm confused. Are you asking for a friendship or more than a friendship? What if this whole thing goes bad?

What if it turns out that we don't really like each other—then how am I supposed to come visit Tamisha?

Okay, that's just crazy. I am not going to throw away a fine guy just because it might not work out between us. Grandma Ruthie says if I can't find anything nice to say, I shouldn't say anything at all. For now, I guess I'd better be quiet.

chapter eighteen

My dad finally leaves the house around noon. He says he has to go get something very important, but he won't tell me what. There's an inkling of hope in me that wonders if he's going to get my car. I know it's just wishful thinking. It'll be a good three months before that happens.

I call Javon with fingers crossed, hoping that he will answer the phone even though he is at work. My wish is granted with, "Yeah."

"Hey!"

"Say, what you up to?" I just know he's cheesin' from ear to ear.

"I'm at my dad's house until later this evening. More drama. I'm tryin' not to take it to the streets with his girlfriend."

Javon saves her face. "Naw, don't do that. That's not your style."

Javon says work is going fine. Since it's cold, things are

slow. That's odd, because I hear people talking, a little music, and the sound of a car's brakes in the background. "Sounds to me like things are pretty busy."

"I'm just . . . on break, you could say."

"Javon, did you get fired?" I fuss.

His voice comes back with a hint of anger. "I told you I'm still workin', right?"

"Yeah."

"Don't trip."

I apologize because I don't want to waste our precious time having an argument. I tell him that I will pray for him so he can keep his job.

"You pray?" He's surprised to the point of whispering a few words of profanity.

"Of course."

"Aw, now I *know* I gotta stop messing with you." He gives a nervous laugh.

"What are you talking about?"

"Hey, I ain't been doin' too good lately. You might want to keep my name away from God right now. He might strike me down."

"Please, Javon. God cares about everybody all the time."

All this talk about God is making me feel guilty about being on the phone. I wish my mom had not said all that stuff about integrity. And now, to *make* me do the right thing, Javon says he has to get back to work, so we end our conversation with my promise to call him again soon. "I'm going back home tonight, so it may be a couple of days. Hold tight, all right? If I don't get to speak to you again soon, Merry Christmas."

"Merry Christmas."

When I finally hang up the phone, I close my eyes and make a deal with the Lord. No more calling people while I'm grounded—unless it is an absolute emergency. The phone rings, and I almost fall off the couch. I pick it up as though it might be God calling to tell me to stay off the phone.

Thank goodness, it's only Shereese. "Give Reginald the phone." *How rude!*

I click my cheek one time. "Nope."

"You are *so* disrespectful, you know."

"Nope."

"Not to mention ghetto." She takes another swing at me through the phone.

I can give her ghetto. "He ain't hrrr. Whatchu want?"

She makes a gagging sound, then fumes, "I know you're trying to get your parents back together—that's why you're getting into all this trouble with your little friends. You need to give it up. It's never gonna happen, Miss Karis. If your daddy *wanted* Janice, he could have her. She's *not* hard to get." I hear her laugh for a second before the click.

Sometimes, I am so slow. I just sat there with my mouth open and let her talk to me that way and hang up before I got the chance to say anything. This is one of those moments where you look back and say, dang, I should have done this or said that. Too late now. How she gon' diss my momma like that? *Nobody* disses my momma but me!

My daddy is so old-fashioned. He doesn't even have caller ID. I start punching the couch's cushions like crazy. I can't believe I just let Shereese clown me *and* my momma like that. This calls for some action.

When dad comes back, he's all smiles. He's got a little black box in his hand, and he rushes to sit next to me on the couch.

Before I have a chance to say anything, he busts out, "Baby girl, I've got the answer to our problems."

"Good, cause Shereese just—"

"I'm gonna ask Shereese to marry me." He opens up the box and all I see is a fat diamond on top of a platinum band. Now *this* is crazy. I'm speechless.

"Takes your breath away, doesn't it?" He's laughing all goofy, and I cannot believe my daddy. *Did he just say he is going to marry Shereese?*

I still haven't said anything. I wish I could cry, but the tears won't come. I'm looking into my father's eyes and wondering what's wrong with him. How could he marry someone who doesn't treat me right? Why is he trying to act like everything is okay when it isn't? All the air goes out of me, and I fall back on the cushions I just finished beating up.

"Karis, I know it's sudden. I . . . I really think this is the solution. I care about Shereese, I care about you, and I care about your mother." Then he tries to make it seem okay. "Your mother didn't want you staying in this house with me and Shereese not married. I really think this will make every woman in my life happy."

He didn't bother to ask me.

"Do me the honors." He grabs a roll of wrapping paper from behind the tree. "Wrap it up for me and put it under the tree for me, okay? There's tape and scissors in the kitchen. I'm going to call Shereese and try to convince her to come over tomorrow." He kisses me on the cheek, snaps the box closed, and throws it into my lap. "Thanks, baby girl."

All I hear now is the moment of laughter Shereese had just before she disconnected our call today. Her laugh replays itself over and over in my head. I'm a zombie as I go into the kitchen with the wrapping paper and this stupid black box. My daddy is getting married to Shereese. I open the box again and look at the symbol of what is sure to be pure chaos for the next I-don't-know-how-many years.

Dang. This ring is tight. I take it out for a closer look. This could be something out of a magazine, it's so bright and shiny. Wait a minute! Where did he get the money for this ring? Didn't he just tell my mother a few days ago that he didn't have money to pay any extra child support; she'd just have to get along like always? My mom is *always* having to get along! Didn't he tell me that he was going to pay off some bills with the money that he *didn't* spend on my car? And why does he cut me off every time I try to tell him something about his no-good, triflin' girlfriend? He doesn't want to know the truth about her. He can't handle the truth! Okay, I know that's a line from an old movie, but for *real*—my dad is straight trippin'.

I'm standing in the kitchen getting madder and madder. This is really all my fault. If I hadn't used that phone and my daddy hadn't had to spend a portion of my car fund, he wouldn't have had so much extra money lying around to buy Shereese this ring. That's right! She wouldn't *have* this ring if it wasn't for me. And since I'm the reason she *has* the ring, I can also be the reason she *doesn't* have the ring. Forget Shereese, and forget my daddy, too! She's some kind of bipolar crazy, and he's too busy trying to look like a big baller to see how crazy she is. They both deserve each other—but she don't deserve this ring, I know that much.

I snatch the ring from the slot and put it into my jacket pocket. The box is black, empty velvet. It's still too cute for her. I look around the kitchen, and my eyes land upon a yellow box that holds the perfect replacement for her ring. Cheerios!

I hop to reach the box and take out one O. Quickly, I place it in the slot and wrap up the box before my father comes back into the kitchen.

I know I'll have to give the ring back, but at this moment, my only regret is that I won't be able to see Shereese's face when she opens this box and sees a ring of wheat in place of platinum. She won't be laughing then.

chapter nineteen

My mom doesn't pick me up until after midnight. My dad says something about her trying to pilfer his time ever since he said he wouldn't give her any more child support money. Usually, my mom tries not to argue with my dad in front of me, but she must be tired tonight, because she lets it go. "I'm not tryin' to get more money out of you—I'm working more *hours* because of you. You understand? Keeping your own child is the *least* you could do, with your cheap, midlife-crisis-havin' self."

She shuts the car door and immediately apologizes to me. "I'm sorry you had to witness such things, Karis. I shouldn't have said that to him. Your daddy and I aren't seeing eye to eye right now, and I think he . . . never mind. This isn't your problem."

I shove my hand inside my pocket and rub the ring. *I got your back, Momma.*

As usual, my mom crashes when we get home. The adrenaline of the evening is still rushing through me, so I turn on the television and catch the last thirty minutes of *It's a Wonderful Life*. My daddy and I used to watch that movie every year, and every year I would cry. Tonight, I cry more than usual.

I'm almost ready to take off my clothes and get ready for bed when the stupid German shepherd next door starts barking again. With the mood I'm in, I am *not* about to listen to this all night. I wipe my tears and blow my nose, trying to take my mind off my father. Then I hear a tap on my window. I pull my jacket around my waist: my body is frozen in fear. I'm getting ready to scream for help when I hear, "Karis! It's me, Javon!"

I fly to the window and find what *would* be the most welcome face on earth under different circumstances. I open the window. "What are you doing here?"

He gives me a silly, boyish grin. "I don't know. I had to see you. Come outside. Let's go somewhere." I'm not often around people who drink, but I do recognize the smell of alcohol on Javon's breath.

"You tryin' to get me killed?" I raise up as I'm saying this and my head hits the bottom of the window's frame. "Ow!"

He laughs at me. "Some things never change."

"Javon, you've been drinking. I'm not going anywhere with you. You shouldn't even be driving!"

He puts his hands on the sill and acts like he's trying to climb into my window. "Let me spend the night here, then."

I peel his hands off. "You betta get down off my window, boy!"

He staggers back, smiling. "So if I die tonight, it'll be on you."

"No, it won't. I didn't tell you to drink and drive."

"Dang, Karis. Why you bein' so mean? I came over here to see you, baby. I've missed you. Don't hardly get to talk to you. Ain't got nothin' to do but drink, since I can't be with you. Dang, you just don't know . . . I'm crazy about you, girl. Told all my homies about you. Told my momma about you. Risk my life to drive over here in the cold to see you, and you treat me so bad." Javon puts his hands over his eyes and starts acting like he's crying. "Mmmm. Karis won't go nowhere with me. She don't love me no mo."

This is *real* crazy. Not to mention hazardous to my health if my mom wakes up.

It's also kinda romantic. Sydney got drunk once and she said that when you get drunk, the truth comes out. Maybe Javon is telling me stuff that he's too ashamed to tell me when he's sober. I knew it! He cares a lot about me; he wants to be with me, I'm on his mind every moment of the day when he's not working. And look at him standing there in his Fubu hat, his denim jacket, red Fubu shirt, and jeans. His skin is such a clear, solid shade of dark brown. When I showed Tamisha his picture on my cell phone, she said he reminded her of Omarion, only with a different mouth.

He brings his beautiful face closer to mine and kisses me. *What is my name?*

"You gon' go with me or what?"

I must have had a bowl of stupid for lunch, because here I am seriously considering his offer. After the day and the night I had, though, I could go with just about anybody anywhere and be happier than at home watching classic movies that remind me of the good ole days.

"I just want to talk," he says, holding up the Boy Scouts' sign of honor.

"I can come sit in the car with you," I compromise.

"Aiight."

Javon helps me down and we walk to his car, which is parked across the street from my house. He opens the door to the backseat. I cross my arms and look him up and down. He says, "It's just so we can be closer, that's all. I promise. I'm not going to try anything."

I take his word and crawl into the backseat of his car. It's different from the last time I was in here. Instead of plain black seats, the car has leopard-print upholstery. I look over into the front seat and see that Javon has a race-car steering wheel, a wood-grain dash, and a new face to his stereo system. "You've really done a lot to this car, huh?"

He nods proudly. "Yeah. I pimped it out."

I can see my mom's bedroom window from here. I should be able to look out for the light in her room.

"So, what did you want to talk about?" I ask.

Javon scoots in closer to me and puts an arm around my shoulder. I lean my head on his chest and snuggle up to him. Now *this* is perfect. Me and my man in his car, just being with each other.

"I've been thinking about you, baby. You know I'm crazy about you, right?"

I sing, "Yeeeees. I'm crazy about you, too, Boo."

He lifts up so that we can face each other. "I can't promise you forever, you know what I'm sayin', but right now—it's just me and you."

"What are you saying?" I need some clarification here. It sounds to me like I'm his temporary girlfriend.

"I'm sayin', I ain't never just chilled and put everything into one girl. I've always had at least two or three other ones on the side, you know?" Javon explains.

It's sad, but I kind of understand him. I've got Marlon on the side, kinda, if I ever get up the nerve to write him back. "Yeah, I understand."

"So, you're ready to make it official, then? Just me and you?" he asks.

Inside, I am jumping for joy! Javon is asking me to be his girlfriend! I have tamed a tiger! I have calmed the savage beast! I have touched his inner teddy bear! "Yes. I'm ready to make this an official relationship." I make a mental note that December 23 will always be our anniversary. No matter what day we get married on, we'll celebrate two days before Christmas as our *real* anniversary.

So much for trying to keep an eye on my mom's bedroom window. Next thing I know, Javon is blocking my view with his face, his lips, his kisses. There must be some kind of mutation class these boys take, because, like Derrick, Javon seems to have eight arms. I ain't gon' lie—at first I am okay with it. My heart is beating all fast and furious, my head feels light. I can hardly breathe.

But then Javon starts trying to make me lean back by pressing his chest on top of me, and I suddenly realize where all this is going. I mean, Javon is cute and all, but I haven't listened to all those lectures my mom gave me about having a baby too soon for nothing.

I break the seal of our kiss and whisper, "Javon."

He ignores me.

Maybe I should say it a little louder. "Javon."

Between kisses, he asks, "What, baby?"

I *love* the way he says *baby*. "I . . . I can't do this."

"Can't do what?"

"This."

He pulls his face away from mine and rubs my bangs off my forehead. "We're only kissing."

Technically, he's right.

So, we start kissing again. Javon's lips make their way down my chin, to the top of my blouse, and he starts trying to unbutton me. This is the moment my mom has been talking about since I was, like, eight years old. I'm all alone with the man I semi-love, he is kissing me, and I'm feeling like woo-*woo*-woo. We are approaching the point of no return when that little voice starts talking again—only this time it sounds just like my mom. *You know good and well you ain't got no business in the backseat of this car with this boy! Just 'cause I can't see you don't mean God can't see you!*

Great! Now I've got God here. People say that right before you die, your whole life flashes in front of you. Well, I'm not dying, but if I go there with Javon, it might be the end of my life as I know it. Questions flash through my mind. What if I got pregnant? What if I got a disease? What if my mom found out and she killed me—how would I survive that?

This runaway train of thought takes over my head. *Toot! Toot!*

"Javon, get up." I try to push him off, but he's not budging. "Javon, it's hot in here!"

He lifts his body an inch and yells at me, "Karis, we are just kissing!"

I yell back, "I don't wanna kiss anymore." I'm trying to sound tough, like I am gonna kick his behind if he doesn't raise up off me, but my voice comes out more like I'm scared.

He screams into my face. "If you don't wanna be with me, why'd you come out of the house? Why'd you get in this car? Why are you wasting my time?" Suddenly, the guy who was about ready to hit Sheila the other night at Applebee's is back.

I cannot believe the ugly words that are comin' out of his beautiful mouth. "Get off of me, Javon. Please."

Javon thinks about my request for a moment. We're looking directly into each other's eyes—mine pleading with his. I realize now that I am totally and completely at his mercy. If he decides not to let me up, I can't do anything about it. He's already got me pinned down, and he's way stronger than me. I can only ask again. "Please, Javon."

Finally, Javon puts his hands on my shoulders and pushes himself back up. I wince, because, actually, that kind of hurt. He runs his hands from his forehead to the back of his head and starts rocking back and forth. He lets out a growl and suddenly starts punching the back of the driver's seat in lieu of my face. Meanwhile, I'm straightening up my clothes and getting ready to bolt out of here.

Javon leans into the corner of the backseat, watching me. When I reach for the back door handle, I'm stopped cold. It won't open.

He flashes a sinister smirk. "Child safety lock."

I quickly haul my body over the seat, face-first. I've got the front door open a little when Javon grabs my ankle. "Wait, wait, Karis . . . don't go . . . hey . . . I got a Christmas gift for you."

I wish I could scream right now, but how will this look when my mom comes outside? Screaming is a last resort. Maybe I can talk him into letting me go. I say calmly, "Javon, let me go."

"Wait! Just listen, okay?" His voice has calmed down a bit.

"Let me go."

"Close the door and then I'll let you go."

Nothing Javon has said tonight has been the truth. I'm only listening now because I am in the front seat and he's in the back. That buys me about two seconds in front of him. I close the door. He keeps his grasp on my ankle.

"Karis, look. I'm sorry, okay? You just look so good. I can't help myself when I'm around you. Plus, I've been drinkin', so, you know. But here. Here's a Christmas present."

I'm holding my body up by my elbows, chest-down on the front seat, when I hear Javon's movements, the flick of his hand, and money starts raining all around me. Twenties, fifties, hundreds. I can't even count it all. I've never seen this much money at one time in my life.

"Merry Christmas, baby."

He releases my ankle and I finally pull the rest of my body to the front seat. I know I should be running back to my room right about now, but I'm in total shock. "Where did you get all this money?"

"I told you—I got a job."

I look back at him. "Javon, you work at a *car wash*! You gotta be doing something wrong to have all this money!"

His face resembles a mad dog as he orders me out of his car. "Hey—sometimes you gotta do what you gotta do! Get outta my car! You always did think you was too good for me! But I see you stopped tryin' to get out this car when I put that cash money in your face. Get out! Betcha if I give you some *money*, you'll stay in this car, huh? We got a name for girls like you."

I scramble to get out of his car and run back across the street to my window. It takes me a few minutes and every bit of energy I have left to boost myself back inside. I close the window behind me, lower the blinds, and draw the curtains closed.

What just happened to me?

I walk to my dresser and see myself in the mirror. My hair is all over my head, my makeup is smeared, my clothes are all messed up, and I barely escaped from the backseat of a car with someone who . . . who I thought loved me until . . . he turned out to be exactly what he always told me he was—a bad boy.

I cover my face with my hands and squeal softly. My heart feels like it weighs twenty pounds and my head could explode at any second. Ten minutes ago, I was totally in love. I followed my heart to Javon's car and he stomped all over it. Now I'm crying so hard I have to remind myself to keep it down because I don't want my mom to wake up.

Maybe the worst part about it all is that I can't call *anyone.* I cry for another half hour while getting ready for bed. *How could he do this to me? What did I do wrong? Am I that stupid when it comes to judging character?* You try to be nice to someone, try to help him out when he's feeling bad about his dad, when he gets fired from his job, when he takes on another job even though he doesn't like what it pays. And what does he do? He gets another illegal job, then he wants to get mad at me for calling him out?

Okay. I'm starting to get mad now. *Who does he think he is?* I gotta give it to him—he is cute. Can't take that away from him. But he ain't nobody! Maybe he was somebody when he was in high school or when he went off to college, but he ain't nobody *now*! Stupid self don't even want to go back to college. I should have known he wasn't my type. He was lucky to be with me, from looking at his ex-girlfriend. Ooh, I can't stand him!

I get a pen from my purse, yank the journal from my top drawer, and write like a madwoman for minutes.

Javon is DIRT and SLIME and I just found that out the hard way—he tried to force himself on me in the back of his car! Okay, I know you wanna know how I was in the back of his car—it's a long story. Just know: Javin is a DOG and an IDIOT and I hope he gets caught doing whatever illegal thing he's doing so he can be off the streets!

Forget you, Javon! I don't need you! I must have been out of my mind for ever talking to you!

I can breathe now. I take out my contacts and rub my burning eyes. I still can't believe it happened. Even after writing two pages about how much I can't stand Javon, it still hurts. I have always promised myself that I would never get so upset about a boy that I can't sleep. Tonight, the promise is broken.

The first thing I do when I wake up on Christmas Eve is read my journal to make sure last night really happened. It's all there. One look at my puffy eyes and I am now 100 percent sure that Javon and I are through. It's not the first time I've broken up with a guy. Or did he break up with me? Either way, I still can't believe how it all went down.

I spend a long time in the bathroom this morning trying to get my eyes to de-puff by applying a warm towel. If my mom would let me wear makeup the way I want to, I could get rid of all the evidence.

My mom calls to me from the other side of the bathroom door. "You all right in there?"

"Yes."

When I finally come out and go to the kitchen so I can eat breakfast, she catches a glimpse of my face. "Karis? You been crying?"

I look down at my bowl of cereal.

My mom stops what she's doing at the counter and stands to the side of me. She puts a hand under my chin and gently raises my face toward hers. As much as I can't stand my mother when she interferes with my life, I love the way her hands feel when she touches my face.

"Karrrrris," she sings my name as she pulls out a chair and sits next to me. "What's wrong?"

My eyes are watering, because I really need to tell somebody about what happened last night. I was so scared in Javon's car. So humiliated. "I'm okay."

"I talked to your father this morning." She sighs. "He told me that he's getting married soon."

Tears start dripping from my eyes, and my mom leans down to hug me. I reach out and squeeze her tightly. Yeah, I'm sad about my dad and Shereese, but I appreciate the security of my mom's embrace this morning for reasons I hope she will never know.

"Karis," she continues, "you're a big girl now. You know that men and women enjoy each other's companionship. Your father has a right to move on with his life. I know your father and I don't see eye to eye on a lot of things. One thing I'm sure of, though, is that no matter what happens, he loves you *very* much. I don't want you worrying about your place in his life, okay?"

I sniff a few times. "Yes, ma'am."

She kisses me on the forehead and goes back to packing her lunch for work. "I'm only working four hours today. I should be back by one. You can invite Tamisha and Sydney over when I get back, since it's Christmas Eve. Maybe it'll do you good to hang out with some of your friends."

Sometimes, my mom is actually okay.

chapter twenty

I call Tamisha to invite her over. "Girl, I've got a *lot* to tell you," I prelude. "It's over between me and Javon."

"What?" she gasps.

"O-V-E-R," I spell it out for her. "Can you come over today when you get off work? I'll have to fill you in."

"I was supposed to do Sydney's hair when I get off work at twelve." She waits for my response.

"Can you call her and ask her to come, too?"

"Karis, I think you should call her yourself."

The questions fall out of my mouth, "Did you talk to her? Does she forgive me? Is she still mad at me?"

"Yes. Kinda. I don't know," Tamisha answers them. "Just call her. If she agrees to come over your house, we can do her hair there. Otherwise, I'll have to catch up with you after the weekend, because my family is going to Michigan for a few days."

"All right. I'll call you back."

This is so crazy! If Sydney won't come, Tamisha won't come. I need my two best friends now more than ever. *God, please let Sydney forgive me!*

I call Sydney's cell phone. I can tell by the way the voice mail picks up that she rejected my call. I call again. She rejects. I send her a text:

> PLZ pick up. I'm so sorry.☹ I need 2 talk 2 u.

I wait for a few minutes, work up my nerve, then try her again.

Sydney answers this time. "What, Karis?"

From the sound of it, I've got maybe thirty seconds to convince Sydney not to hang up on me. "Look, I'm sorry about what happened, okay? I'm really, really sorry. We've been friends for, like, ever, Sydney, dang."

She hesitates. "I can't tell. You left me hangin'. Friends don't do that to friends."

"Sydney, I'm sorry, okay? I just got scared and panicked. I didn't know what to do."

"How you think *I* felt?" she asks.

I think about it for a moment and concede, "Scared, too."

We wait for a moment in awkward silence. What else can I say? Sydney's really not one to hold grudges for days and weeks. Either she's going to be my friend again or she's going to call it quits and move on.

Slowly, she grumbles, "I heard your parents took away the car."

I breathe again, thankful that Sydney is ready to forgive me. We both lament about the consequences of our actions for a few minutes. Sydney owns up to the fact that she told me the wrong time, and I take responsibility for agreeing to use Angelique's phone. We both know we were wrong.

After we put the phone situation to rest, I tell Sydney that she and Tamisha are welcome to come to my house this afternoon so they can do hair and we can all catch up.

My bedroom has been converted to a beauty shop. We've got music playing, magazines strewn across the room, each of us has a glass of Coke, and we're sharing a big bowl of Cool Ranch Doritos. First, Tamisha braids in brown Yaky hair in the front to make about an inch of cornrows. She then glues in some more tracts, swoops the whole thing up to the top, and creates an anchor for a ponytail. Then she wraps and pins spiral tracks around the base until Sydney has a full, flowing ponytail that will move with every step she takes down the basketball court. Sydney makes Tamisha cut it shorter so that it won't get in the way. I make it sound easy, but it's all very complicated. The whole process takes no less than ninety minutes, which gives us plenty of time to talk about last night.

"Okay, now back this thing up for a minute," Sydney says, grilling me for the dirty details. "While you were in the backseat of the car—"

"Shhh!" I point toward my mom's bedroom.

She lowers her voice. "What *exactly* happened?"

"I already told you. We kissed. I drew the line, though, when he tried to lay on me. I made him get up."

Sydney cross-examines. "You say he *tried* to lay on top of you and you made him get *up*."

"Yes."

"Well, if he *tried* to lay on you but was unsuccessful in assuming this position, why did you have to make him get *up* if he was never *lying* on *top* of you the first place?"

I cock my head to the side and say point-blank, "Sydney, nothing happened."

She throws her hands up and relents. "Just makin' sure you're still one of us."

"If it was me," Tamisha interjects, "I would have kicked him between the legs so hard, his kids would come out with my footprint on their foreheads!"

Sydney falls over laughing, but I can only manage a slight grin. I've said all kinds of things about how I wouldn't let this or that happen when I was with a boy. Everything happened so fast last night, I didn't have time to think about kicking Javon where it hurts. I froze. Maybe that's the part that scares me most. When push came to shove, I couldn't kick him, I couldn't call for help, I couldn't do anything except beg him to stop.

"If you ask me," Tamisha adds, "Javon was trouble from the beginning. Why was he hanging around a driver's ed parking lot trying to pick up high school girls anyway? Can't he find someone his own age to mess with?"

I buck my eyes out in disbelief. "Hello! Weren't you the one who told me, and I quote, go for it?"

Tamisha smiles and squints her eyes. "Did I say that?"

"Yes!"

She pulls her neck in like a turtle. "Oops! Sorry."

"Apology accepted. And trust me, I won't be doing anything anytime soon. I obviously don't even know how to pick guys yet."

"Me, either," Tamisha admits. "The ones I really like don't

like me, and the ones who like me are . . . something's wrong with 'em."

"Oh, that is not true!" Sydney counters. "Emmitt Hampton liked you, and there is definitely nothing wrong with that fine young specimen!"

"His name is *Emmitt*. I can't be with an *Emmitt*. Come on now—Emmitt and Tamisha? How that sound?"

"You find something wrong with *everybody*, Tamisha." I have to side with Sydney on this one. "You ain't had a boyfriend since we were freshmen. What's up with you?"

"I'm not one for games." Tamisha wipes her hand on a towel and eats a few Doritos. "If I do get a boyfriend, he ain't gonna go to Central, that's for sure. And he's gotta have a job, 'cause I ain't supporting no man."

"What if he plays sports so he can't work?" Sydney stands up for athletes everywhere, but Tamisha is not persuaded.

Tamisha sticks up her thumb and points it. "To the left, to the left."

This calls for Beyoncé's "Irreplaceable." Tamisha takes a break, and we all dance in front of the mirror, lip-synching the song. Due to my recent breakup, I'm the lead singer. It was silly, but I felt so good when we finished that song. *I didn't need Javon—he needed me!*

"Okay," Sydney says as she pulls a pad and pencil from her purse, "we gotta come up with some kind of ground rules for relationships with boys."

"That's crazy," I argue. "You can't tell your heart who to fall in love with."

"Au contraire, mon frère," Sydney says.

"Mon amie," I correct her. "I'm not your brother—I'm your friend." That French II comes in handy every now and then.

"Duly noted. Nerd."

The closest thing I can find to hurl at Sydney is a pillow. She ducks, picks it up, and throws it back at me. I should have known I wouldn't be quick enough to hit her.

"As I was saying," she continues as though she's talking to a room full of jurors and spectators, "we need clear criteria, because Karis here let a mentally unstable loser slide past her radar, and Tamisha is throwing away a perfectly good guy because of the name his parents so erroneously gave him."

"And what about you!" Tamisha forces Sydney to look into the mirror. "Your last prospect already had a girlfriend!"

"I was not about to get with Avery McWilliams!"

"Oh, please! You called me—matter of fact, it's because you called me that I ended up in trouble in the first place! That was the day my mom read my journal!"

Sydney won't take the blame for that one. "No, no! Let the record show: I told you that it was a bad idea to go to Derrick's house!"

"Anyway!" I blow her off. Sydney is always trying to change the subject when it comes to her and boys. If you ask me, I think she's still strung out on this guy named Patrick that she fell head over heels with when we were in eighth grade. His parents divorced, and Patrick moved back to Chicago. She has been somewhat single since then.

"Okay," Sydney fesses up, "I have been a serial single for two years."

Tamisha coughs up the name. "Patrick."

Sydney rolls her eyes at Tamisha. "I heard that. Anyway, let's come up with a . . . what's that thing teachers use for writing? A matrix with numbers and descriptions—"

"A rubric?" I ask.

"Yes! A guy rubric, or a test, or something. We can't just be going through life without some kind of guidelines, you know?" Sydney suggests.

Sydney is already numbering one through ten on her paper. She puts blanks beside each number. "Ten points each; seventy is passing," she decides. "Okay, what's number one?"

I blurt out the first thing that comes to mind. "Looks."

"That is not number one," Tamisha shouts. "That's how you got in this mess with Javon in the first place."

"I have to think about my kids," I reason. "I don't want my kids to come out looking all ugly. Besides, you have to have *some* kind of attraction to the person, or it just won't work out. I read that in an article online—gotta have chemistry."

"Well, since everything is ten points each, it doesn't matter if that's number one or number ten," Sydney declares, clearing that one up for us. "Let's call it attractiveness instead of looks so it doesn't sound so shallow."

"But what if he's cute with no job?" Tamisha asks. "You can be cute all day, but a brother starts lookin' real ugly to me when I have to pay for his food."

"Number two—job," Sydney declares as she adds it to the list. "Can we substitute job with extracurricular activities?"

Tamisha sticks out her lips for a no, but I am with Sydney on this one. "Sports, job, church functions, volunteer work, or he's in the top ten percent of his class. Basically, he can't be sitting at home all day every day after school doin' nothin'."

"What if he already finished high school?" Sydney thinks of everything.

"College," Tamisha and I say simultaneously.

"College—number three."

By the time we finish, Sydney has added all of her legal

mumbo-jumbo talk (at least what she knows of it) to our practically publishable list. It covers everything that a young woman should consider when considering a young man for a relationship. We argue over some of the specifics, but we end up agreeing that these are now in stone. I copy it into my journal:

Dear Me:

Here are the rules of love for Sydney, Tamisha, and me (in the form of a quiz). If a guy doesn't get at least 7/10, he's out of the picture.

The Boyfriend Quiz

1. Attractiveness—He must be attractive enough to produce chemistry, thusly contributing to the kindling of romance. If he becomes unattractive due to no fault of his own (i.e., accidents, sports injury) and the relationship has already begun, this rule can and should be waived.

2. Job—He must have a job, be involved in extracurricular activities, volunteer, be in the top 10% of class, or be otherwise occupied with (legal) responsibilities outside of school so that he is not sitting around living a life of laziness and leisure.

3. Ambition—He must be enrolled in a college and be passing said courses. If he is a full-time student, rule #2 does not apply. If he is a part-time student, rule #2 applies. Military enlistment qualifies as a full-time occupation.

4. Kids—He cannot have any kids. This rule is set for review by Sydney, Tamisha, and Karis in fifteen years, should either of us still be single.

5. Spiritual—He must believe in God and share common religious beliefs if a relationship is to be pursued.

6. Record—He can have no criminal record and shall not engage in any criminal activity. Involvement in illegal activity will result in immediate termination of the relationship.

7. Demeanor—He must present himself well before friends and family; he must not exhibit any violent tendencies or mental instability, and he must have common sense.

8. Substances—He cannot use alcohol or drugs, except prescribed by a physician. If he is over 21, he may drink casually—but not drive—if religiously acceptable.

9. Treatment—He must treat me like a queen at all times, showing sincere concern for my well-being.

10. Fidelity—He must cease from romantic involvement with other females once the relationship has been declared exclusive by mutual agreement. Even after said exclusivity is declared, he must allow sufficient space for me to grow and have my own life as an individual.

*Forgiveness and reconciliation clause—He can be forgiven for infrequent violation of the rules if he acknowledges his mistake, apologizes voluntarily, and makes sincere effort to avoid repeating the mistake.

Karis Ready-to-Grade Reed

For practice, we decide to size up Javon on the quiz. He gets a forty.

"That's an F minus!" Sydney shrieks. "See! Now this quiz is research-based. We should sell this thing, I'm telling you!"

Later, when I'm alone, I'll have to score Marlon.

chapter twenty-one

With the hair and the boyfriend quiz out of the way, we are now free to address my second topic of tragedy: my dad, Shereese, and my living arrangements. I don't know what time my dad plans to propose to Shereese, but I know it won't be long before I'm busted.

"Aren't you scared?" Sydney asks. "My dad would totally lose it if I did something like that!"

"I am scared—but right now, I've got nothing to lose. I'm not getting a car, my dad is getting married to the Wicked Witch of the West, my mom kinda wants to kick me out, and I have no man. What else could happen to me?"

I've heard people say *"Speak of the devil and he shall appear."* I know my daddy ain't the devil, but when we start talking about it, my cell phone rings with my dad's number on the screen. I don't answer. He calls again. Twice.

"Sounds like somebody found a Cheerio," Sydney cooes.

The house phone rings and my mom answers it. I'm counting down from ten. My mother makes it to my room at two. "Karis, your father would like to speak to you."

I follow my mother into the hallway and close the door behind me. Either Sydney or Tamisha turns down the music so they can hear everything.

"Hello."

"What did you do with the ring? And why? Do you have any idea how embarrassing that was for me *and* Shereese?" His voice is getting louder with each question. "Do you think this is some kind of joke? Do you think this is how people work out their problems—stealing rings and putting food in the box?"

"I didn't *steal* the ring."

"You took it out if this house without permission, Karis. You *stole* it."

I look up at my mom and notice the slight upturn in the corner of her lips. She's trying in vain to hide it with her left hand. With my mom listening in on the conversation, I should tell my dad everything now so I won't have to repeat myself. "The reason I took the ring is because Shereese was talkin' smack on the phone to me. She talked about momma, she talked about me, and she even talked about *you* the first time she and I got into it. Plus, it ain't right for you to spend child support money on a wedding ring."

My dad stutters a bit and tries to throw me off. "What I do with Shereese is between me and her, and anything having to do with child support is between me and your momma!"

"No, Daddy. I'm a part of all this!" My leftover tears from last night come back. "What happens to Momma happens to me, and what you decide affects me, too! If you marry Shereese, she's gonna make me *and* you miserable!"

He resorts to his usual solution. "Put your momma back on the phone!"

My mom is looking me in the eye like *I ain't mad at you.* Of course, she can't say so, because it probably wouldn't be right. She assures my father she'll drop off the ring first thing in the morning, on her way to work. When she hangs up, she blinks one time and asks, "Did you mean everything you said to your father just now?"

"Yes."

"Is that what really happened?"

I nod. "I got mad at him because Shereese is disrespectful, and she said some really jacked-up stuff about me and you. When he showed me the ring he'd bought for her . . . I don't know . . . I just lost it for a minute. I thought about you working so much and him saying he didn't have any extra money, and I knew he must not have been telling the whole truth. If he had money to buy a ring for that . . . *girl,* he could have helped you out a little this month. And then on top of all that, he asked *me* to wrap it for her! I couldn't do it, Momma. I just couldn't."

Finally, my mother sighs. "Karis, you may have felt that you had valid reasons to be angry with your father, but what you did was wrong. As far as child support goes, that's grown folks' business. Let me and your father work those things out between ourselves, okay? He and I talked later about the money situation, after we had both calmed down. We got that whole thing straight.

"And as for his love life, your father is a grown man with a free will. He can marry whomever he chooses. You are not responsible for his actions; you are only responsible for your response to his actions. You have to give the ring back to your father so that he can give it to Shereese; you can't stop him."

"I know." My head hangs from my neck like a flag from a pole.

For the second time today, my mother lifts it. "I know it's hard, honey."

"She said some really bad things about us, Momma."

My mother crosses her arms and pulls her neck back. "You think I let what people say about me get under my skin? 'How she gon' talk to young girls about abstinence when she got pregnant at sixteen?' 'She ain't nothin' but a hypocrite!' 'She ain't no example to be holdin' up in front of these young girls.' Ha! I wish I had a dime for every time somebody talks about me! It doesn't bother me anymore. I let it slide off my back like water off a duck." My mother's eyes turn to slits, and she lifts her left eyebrow. "But the next time she says something, let me know. You don't have to be subjected to verbal abuse by an adult. I'll take it up with your father myself. Got it?"

"Yes, ma'am."

She breathes fresh air into the conversation. "It's nice to know that you appreciate all the hard work I do to support you."

"You be *ballin'*, Momma! Cash money!"

She smiles and waves me off. "I be *workin'*! And now I'm about to be *sleepin'*! Good night. Tell your friends to call home and check in with their parents after a while."

"Okay."

She stops in her tracks and turns back to me. "And, Karis?"

"Yes?"

"I appreciate you telling me the whole truth. Shows a lot of integrity."

When I step back into my room, Sydney and Tamisha give me high fives. We turn the music back up as the salon nears a close. "Shereese don't deserve a Cheerio. You should have put some Hy-Top cereal in that mug," Tamisha suggests with a cackle.

"Loop of Cheer," Sydney snorts.

I add, "Cheeri-Q."

"That's corny, Karis. Change subject."

I fall onto my bed in laughter. It's so good to have friends who make you laugh when your heart is aching.

"Let's see this ring," Sydney commands, shimmying her shoulders. "I wanna see what this fuss is all about."

I guess it can't hurt to take one last look at the thing before I give it back. I walk toward my closet, grab my jacket from the closet rod, feel the left pocket. No ring. Must be the right pocket. Still no ring. I put my hand inside each pocket again. Same results—no ring! "Oh, snap! The ring is gone!" I exclaim.

Tamisha slaps her hand on the CD player and stops the music. "What?"

All the air has been pushed out of my body. "It's gone! I had it right here in this jacket last night before—"

Sydney finishes my sentence, "—you got into Javon's car!"

My eyes must be ten inches in diameter. "It must have fallen out while we were in the car or when I climbed over the seat! Dang! I gotta get that ring back!"

"Call Javon." Tamisha takes charge of the situation, which is actually what she does best.

"I don't want to talk to him, and he's not gonna talk to me!" I argue.

Tamisha give me a "duh" look. "How else are you going to get the ring back?"

"I don't know. Even if he does talk to me, I don't know how I'm going to get into the back of his car again without getting attacked!" I might not get so lucky if I try that again.

Sydney's naïveté speaks. "Just call him and tell him you left something very important in his car."

Tamisha and I both look at Sydney like she's crazy.

"So he can find the ring and go pawn it?" Tamisha fills Sydney in on the reality of dealing with money-hungry thugs. "He's not a reasonable person, Sydney. Need I remind you— he only got a forty on the boyfriend quiz?"

I squeeze my eyes shut and throw my head back. "Why do these things always happen to me?"

"Okay," Tamisha says, "here's what we're gonna do. Call Javon. Tell him that you made a big mistake. Tell him you'd like to see him again. Alone."

"What if he tries something again?" I swear, I cannot get back in that car.

"You tell him"—Tamisha pauses to think for a second—"tell him you want to pick up right where you left off last night."

"Alright, Tamisha, that's good," Sydney approves. "I like the sound of that."

I don't.

"We'll meet Javon somewhere. You will get back into his car while Sydney and I wait in my car. We won't let you out of our sight. We'll call you every three minutes. And when you've got the ring, you answer and say yes. Then we'll come over to the car and bust you out."

"Bust me out? How? That's crazy!"

"Look, we gotta do something crazy if we're gonna get this ring back," Tamisha says. She's right about that much.

I call Javon four times before he finally returns. "Whatchu want?"

Just hearing him makes my flesh crawl. I don't think I can go through with it. Sydney mouths, "Do it!"

"Javon, I was thinking . . . I'm really sorry about last night. I acted like an immature little girl. I really like you, and I want to . . ."

Tamisha mouths, "Pick up."

"Pick up where we left off. Do you think you could meet me at—"

I'm shaking my hand, begging Tamisha and Sydney to give me a location. We hadn't gotten that far in the plan. Sydney stands up and starts acting like she's shooting hoops.

I guess, "The basketball court?" Sydney nods because I just won at charades.

The smile in Javon's voice makes me sick to my stomach. "Now *that's* my girl. I mean—my *woman*. I got a little more business to handle, but I can meet you at six."

"Okay," I agree. I must be crazy.

chapter twenty-two

I leave a note for my mom that Tamisha, Sydney, and I are going to pick up a gift—which is, by the way, not a total lie. I don't really know whether or not my mom would give me permission to leave, but hopefully, I'll never have to know. Just in case she wouldn't, Sydney, Tamisha, and I leave the house very quietly.

We do a cell phone check on the way to the basketball court. All phones are charged, working fine. I've seen those episodes of cop shows where somebody is wired to record a conversation with the bad guys. Those stings always go wrong. So what makes us think we can do a better job than the television professionals?

God, this is crazy. Please don't let Javon—or my momma—get me! Tamisha is calm, cool, and collected as she commandeers this mission to recover Shereese's ring. Sydney is also in the front seat playing detective, writing down Javon's license plate as we approach him in the parking lot next to the courts. "Just in case he takes off with you in the car and we lose you in traffic," she says, trying to comfort me but actually scaring me half to death.

Javon is waiting for me, leaning up against his Impala. "He *is* cute," Sydney remarks.

I yell, *"Irrelevant!"*

"I'm just sayin'."

"Stop sayin'," Tamisha barks. "Karis, get out."

"Wait," I squeal. I have to pray first.

Sydney huffs, "Oh, come on already!"

"No. I'm serious. Bow your heads," I command. "Father God, I am so sorry about everything I have done wrong, but right now, I need Your help. I don't know how You are going to work this out. I just . . . need You. And thank You for my friends, too. Amen."

Tamisha unlocks the doors of her Nissan Sentra and I step out of the car and walk toward Javon awkwardly. I look down at my white baby-doll T-shirt, blue jeans, and black Nike shoes, wondering how this ensemble will hold up if I have to jump out of a moving car.

It's cold and getting dark outside. There are only a few guys left shooting hoops. I'm relieved to see someone other than me, Sydney, and Tamisha within the vicinity. If things don't go as planned, maybe those guys will come help us.

Javon opens the backseat door again. I can't start my search there. "You mind if we sit in the front and talk first?" He shrugs as though I'm wasting his time. My feelings are hurt, but I can't think about my heart right now. I'm trying to have a conversation while keeping an eye on my friends. Tamisha and Sydney circle the block in Tamisha's car and park where I can see them on the other side of the blacktop.

Once I've got my girls in sight, I start looking for the ring. It's so dark that I can't see anything. I'm gonna have to feel for it. Javon reaches across the center and puts his hand around my shoulder. "What did you want to talk about?"

"Us."

"What about us?"

I'm reaching between the seat cushion behind me, trying to keep eye contact with Javon the whole time. No ring. I say the first thing that comes to my mind. Anything to keep him from watching my hands. "About our relationship. I really hope you won't use me, Javon. Guys like you have a habit of hurting girls like me."

"I'm almost nineteen years old. I'm ready to settle down with someone. She can't be actin' like no little girl, though. If you gon' be down with me, be *down*. Since you came here tonight, I know you're for real. I know you love me. I love you, too, Karis."

How can he lie to my face like this?

My hands stop moving. All my teenage life I've waited for a guy to tell me he loves me, and here it is—a total lie—spoken while I'm trying to locate a stolen ring in his car. *This is so sad!*

My phone rings, snapping me back to reality. It's Tamisha. "You got it?"

"No. Call me later."

I hang up and shriek, "Ow!" I bend down and pretend to scratch my leg with one hand and feel around on the floor with the other. "You got ants in this car?"

"No. What's wrong with you?"

"I'm itchin'. Ow!" I move my foot further up the footboard so I can search under the seat a little. I bend over so much that I drop my cell phone on the floor, giving me opportunity to reach under the seat a little further. No ring.

His hands start sliding down my back, and I pop up like a jack-in-the-box. "I'm okay!" I announce to Javon. "I'm okay. Let's go in the backseat."

My cell phone rings again. "Did you find it?"

"Oh, hey. Naw, but I'm busy right now. I gotta get back with you. Aiight." I snap the phone shut and give Javon a tentative smile. This is playing out like a *That's So Raven* episode, only there's no studio audience laughing at my silly antics, and I don't have a clue what the future holds.

Javon unlocks the doors so we can get out and get in the backseat. I'm using every second of light to visually search the backseat. Nothing. "Ooh! Did you see that?"

"What?"

"I thought I saw an . . . ant on the floor." I keep my door open so the dome light shows and I can get low to search. *Man, where is that ring?*

"Karis, what is wrong with you? Did you come here to get serious or to play?" Javon's temper is flaring, and I've gotta do something quick. I close the door behind me, and it's déjà vu. I'm trying to figure out a way to keep his hands off me and, at the same time, keep *my* hands moving between the seats. *How do I get myself into these messes!* I can't do two things at once. He's pressing his whole body down onto me when I call off the search.

"Wait, Javon," I say as I push up on his chest.

"What?" I can tell by the vein popping out in his forehead that he's aggravated. Javon looks at me suspiciously. "What is up with you? Just relax."

Then he kisses me softly and my body is acting like it forgot about the ring mission. Thankfully, Tamisha doesn't forget. She calls again.

"Who are all these dudes callin' you?" Javon says in an accusatory tone.

"These are my friends. The ones who dropped me off."
I answer, "Hello?"

"Do you have the ring?" Tamisha asks.

"No."

"Hurry up. I'm giving you three more minutes."

I hang up the phone again. "Javon, my friends are coming back to pick me up. Tamisha has to hurry up and get home. Let's just—ow! You have ants in the backseat, too!" I check the seat cushions one last time.

"Naw, I ain't got no ants, and we ain't got much time, baby, come on."

He pulls me into him and kisses me roughly on the lips. I try to push him back, but he's too strong. "Javon, stop it."

He pushes me away from him. "Why are you here?"

I can't find the ring. I know Javon is stupid and extremely attracted to me right now, but I'm so desperate that I don't know what else to do except confess. "Javon, I can't find Shereese's ring. I think it fell out of my jacket last night when I was in this car."

"Why didn't you just tell me that?"

"Because of the way you acted last night!"

He leans over and sticks his hand underneath the front driver's seat. "I found it!"

I gasp in delight! I promise I can forget about all the bad things he has done and start all over again! "Thank you, Javon!"

He raises up and smiles at me. "Here it is."

I follow his hand as he brings it to the ray of light streaming from the basketball court. I don't see a ring. What I see is his middle finger sticking straight up at me. Javon falls back in laughter as my face melts.

"You are so stupid!" I scream at him.

He's laughing so hard he can hardly speak. I stumble over into the front seat, barely able to keep from crying. As I'm getting out of the car, he adds insult to injury. "When I *do* find it, I'm keepin' it! I'll give it to a *real* woman!"

I slam the door and run toward Tamisha's car. The sound of my feet thumping against the pavement is welcomed. I'm out of that car, I was not assaulted, and I'm free of Javon forever.

"What happened?" Tamisha screams as she takes note of my face.

I slither inside her car and motion for her to start driving. "I didn't find it," I manage to explain. "And Javon says that if he finds it, he'll give it to someone else."

"You told him?" from Sydney.

"I didn't have a choice. I couldn't find it. I needed his help." The fear and disappointment of the evening have smashed me, emotionally. My tears are coming so quickly that they blur my vision. I try my best not to cry in front of people, but there's no way I can stop these emotions from taking over my eyes, my nose, and my facial expressions. It's good to have friends who don't care how ugly I get when I'm having a meltdown, which is exactly what I'm going through at the moment.

When we get back to my house, we decide that we should all go in together so my mom will believe the note, if she happens to be up. For the next fifteen minutes, my friends and I make a last-minute effort to find the ring in my room. Sydney is lifting things so that she can search the floor, I'm looking through my jewelry box, and Tamisha is looking through my junk drawer. We're scrambling here and there, making all kinds of noise, when Tamisha says, "Hey. What's this?"

My heart stops and I turn to face her, hoping that she has found the little rock and band that hold the key to my future. When my eyes make it down to her hand, I can only wonder how things just keep getting worse and worse for me. She's holding the letter from Marlon in her hand.

"Why is my brother writing you?" she asks.

I am so broken down right now, I can't even begin to think of an excuse for why Marlon is writing me. Out with the truth. "He . . . just . . . wrote me."

"I *see* that, but *why* is he writing you?" she demands.

"He just wants a friend."

"I thought you said you hadn't gotten the letter from Iraq yet."

"I said I hadn't received a letter from Marlon's friend," I recall for her.

She glares at me and hisses, "Same difference. You lied, Karis."

"I did not lie to you, Tamisha."

Sydney interjects, "She's right, Tamisha. Technically, she did not lie to you."

"Shut up, Sydney. This isn't a courtroom." Sydney makes a motion to zip her lips, then Tamisha keeps biting into me. "I wanna know why you felt you had to keep this from me? Is it because you know *I* know how much of a player you are, how selfish you are?"

Tamisha throws the letter onto the ground and approaches me. She crosses her arms, awaiting my response.

"I would never do anything to hurt Marlon, Tamisha, and you know it. He's not asking me for a relationship—he just wants a friend," I repeat.

"Well, I certainly wouldn't recommend you—especially knowing how much you like to keep secrets and all. He could find a much better friend than you."

"See, this is why I didn't want to tell you. This is why *Marlon* didn't come out and tell you—you trip when it comes to him."

"He's my brother!" she exclaims.

Sydney is sitting on my bed watching us like she's at a tennis match; her face going from left to right, right to left.

"Marlon is like a brother to me—*and* Sydney," I say.

Sydney coughs to bring attention to herself and throw in her two cents. "I never wanted Marlon for a brother."

Tamisha looks at Sydney like she's crazy. "What's that supposed to mean?"

"I'm sorry, Tamisha—your brother is way fine."

Tamisha rolls her eyes back toward me. "Is that what you think, Karis? You think Marlon is fine? You wanna get with him after you've been with all these losers like Javon and Derrick?"

"Wait a minute," Sydney intervenes, "get real, Tamisha. Your brother is eighteen years old. He has a right to pick his own friends. Why are you trippin' so hard?"

Tamisha lets her neck roll to one side as she looks me up and down. "From what I can tell, my brother is too good for you. The last thing he needs right now is a *fake* friend who's so busy trying to lie and cheat her way through life that she wouldn't recognize a good guy if he came up and kissed her smack on the lips."

Why me? How am I already onto another case of drama when I haven't even resolved the situation with the ring yet? This is a mess within a mess, and I cannot deal with it right now without saying something I will probably regret later. "Look, I'm sorry I didn't tell you, okay? But can we just table this for now, Tamisha?"

"Sounds like a plan to me. I gotta get home anyway," Sydney mumbles.

Tamisha gives me the evil eye and walks toward my bedroom door to leave.

Sydney offers a bit of consolation. "I'm sorry we couldn't help you get the ring back."

"Well, you did try," I respond, giving them credit for their friendship.

I really want to tell them Merry Christmas as they walk out the door, but I can't do it. This is the *Un*merriest Christmas ever. This is a nightmare. Tomorrow morning, my life is over. My mom won't buy the "I lost it" excuse. She knows I'd never do something so stupid—unless I was stupid enough to get in the backseat of a car with a total idiot boy. I want to have integrity, but I don't see how the truth could help me now.

I spend the next hour searching my room one more time. Nothing.

I'm never gonna see that ring again, which means I'm never getting a car, which means I'll never have a life. I'm gonna be sick.

I crawl into bed and pray. "Father God, I don't know what to say. I just need You to do something. I'm really sorry about all this stuff with Javon. Up until now, I thought I knew everything. Well, neither You nor my momma has to tell me: I don't. If it means anything, I feel bad about everything. I want to start doing the right things, with integrity or whatever. It's hard, though. Even praying is hard right now. Please, Lord, work something out."

At church, they're always saying that no one knows when Christ will return. "He'll come in the twinkling of an eye, like a thief in the night," I've heard. "And when He comes, there will be no more trouble."

I hope tonight is the night.

chapter twenty-three

No such luck. The world is, apparently, still turning. I barely slept last night, so I'm surprised when I open my eyes and see light. I guess my body just gave out on me and I did sleep after all. It takes maybe ten seconds to feel the weight of the world press down on me with the realization of what's going to happen today. Not only will I have to tell my parents that I don't have the ring, I'll also have to explain why I don't have the ring, because I can't think of a lie good enough to get me out of this one.

What's funny is, I really don't want to lie. Call me crazy, but it felt really good yesterday when I told my mom exactly why I took Shereese's ring. It also felt good when my mom said that she appreciated my integrity. I wish I could go back to two days ago and start over again. I would never take the ring, I wouldn't get in the car with Javon, and I wouldn't be here wondering how to get out of this mess.

My mom is up and getting ready. She's in the shower. I've got about thirty minutes tops to write my eulogy and bequeath all of my precious belongings to my friends and family.

My legs don't want to get out of bed. I have to force them to the floor and toward my dresser. I see myself in my mirror and realize that I'm still wearing the clothes I had on yesterday. I thought I looked bad yesterday morning, but I was wrong. My makeup is smeared, and my eyes are red because I slept in my contacts. I can smell my funk and I haven't even raised my arms. This is what bad kids must look like. Street hustlers. Vandals. Computer hackers. I'm not *that* bad, am I?

I close my eyes and attempt to pray one more time, but there's nothing left to say. Obviously, God is not tryin' to hear me right now. I have to move on. It's time to make up a realistic lie. The setting of the lie has to be outside, because that's the only way I can place the ring beyond a location where we can actually find it.

Outside. Outside.

Outside!

It's a long shot, I know, but I didn't look outside when I was searching for the ring. Maybe it fell out somewhere between the car and my bedroom. I scramble over to my window and take a deep breath. After the stunt my friends and I pulled with Javon last night and the time we spent tearing up my room, I don't want to get my hopes up about finding the ring now. Slowly, I open the window and look below. Nothing. I knew it was futile. I'm just about to close the window when something—a tiny flash—catches my eye. I blink twice, following the glimmer. I blink again and squint my eyes until they're almost closed. Oh. My. God. *Thank you, God!* There, glistening in the grass below, sits the most beautiful sight I will ever see in a million years: the ring! The ring! This is the best day of my life! Instead of just thinking it, I say it out loud this time. "Thank you, God!"

I climb out the window, jump down, and pick up the ring. My heart is racing wildly. Yes! I can have my life back! I kiss the ring, and I throw it back into the room. I watch it land on my bed—I don't want to let this ring out of my sight for one second. Then I place both hands on the windowsill and hoist myself back up into the room. In an instant, I lose my balance and the top half of my body falls over onto the bed. I'm trying to get control of things, but my right foot catches the curtain and—*wham!*—the blinds, the curtains, and the rod come tumbling down. *This is not happening!*

In a whirl of hot pink sheers, I still manage to get everything in except my left leg, but it's too late. My mom opens the door. "Karis? Are you okay in here?"

Silence. Calm before the storm. My mom shifts her weight to one side and crosses her arms. "Oh, it's so very nice of you to come back home after a night of doing God-knows-what with God-knows-who." Her voice is soft. Almost a whisper.

"Momma, it's not—"

"SAVE IT!" Her eyes are wider than I've ever seen them, her neck is strained to capacity, and her face is twisted with anger. She storms out of my bedroom and I hear her doing something in the kitchen. I need to unravel myself from these curtains, 'cause I have no idea what she's about to do to me. I listen for her footsteps. By the time she returns to the room, I'm on my feet. At least for now.

She throws a gob of trash bags at me. "Pack. Your. Stuff."

"But Momma—"

"But Momma nothin'! If you want to stay out all night, you ain't got to try to sneak back in! Go on and stay out there! You don't want to live here and follow my rules, LEAVE! I ain't gon' stop you! Go live in sin with your daddy and his girlfriend—you'll fit right in!"

I look at her and see nothing but rage and pain in her face—the line between her eyebrows, her nostrils flaring. And behind all of that, eyes that can hardly contain the growing well of tears.

"What you waitin' on? Pack this stuff up or I'll give it all to Goodwill!"

I fall to my knees, open the top drawer, and begin putting my clothes into the bag, one item at a time. My mom takes two steps over to the dresser, pulls the entire top drawer out, and flips it over. My clothes cascade to the floor. "Move faster!"

Handful after handful, I begin stuffing clothes into the plastic bag. I'm moving as quickly as possible, but it seems like this is happening in slow motion. I cannot believe that my mother is kicking me out—like this!

She's dumping the second and third drawer now. "I try to give you everything, Karis! Everything you ask for so you won't have to go out tryin' to get it from some boy or from your friends. I've tried to be a good mother to you—and this is how you repay me! Huh? Staying out all night?"

My closet is next on the hit list. My mother hugs a section of my clothes, lifts them off the pole, and throws them on top of the pile she already made. It's actually pretty violent, from my perspective. All the while, she's fussing at me. "I don't understand! You *know* how hard things are for us! You *know* how hard it is to be a single mom, but you just ain't gon' be happy 'til it happens to you! Or AIDS or drugs or goin' to jail!"

This may be my chance. I hold my head down and speak softly. "I'm not—"

"Don't talk to me! Pack it or leave it! You got five minutes to meet me in the car! Five minutes! Whatever ain't got packed by then, that's just too bad! I will not be late to work on account of you!" My mother kicks my clothes out of her way as she leaves my room.

"This is some Christmas gift, Karis!"

A minute later, she starts the car in the driveway.

My hands move quickly to fill the bags, and the tears come down my face like rain. *She won't even listen to me!* I can hardly see what I'm doing. Grab and shove, grab and shove. After the third trash bag, I hear her blow the horn for me to come out. I wipe my eyes and look around my room. I toss my CDs into bag #2, my contact lens stuff in bag #1, and I put the ring in my pocket.

She blows the horn again. I grab a pair of Nikes and some boots, and push them down into bag #3. This is all I can carry. I throw my purse over one shoulder and struggle down the hallway, wondering if this will be the last time I'll be in my house. My mom meets me at the front door, grabs one of the bags, and throws it into the trunk as carelessly as possible. I put the other two in the backseat while she goes back to lock the front door.

When we're both in the car, she demands, "Give me your key."

The dam breaks. I'm crying like crazy as I reach into my purse and give her the key to the only place I have ever called home. *This is not fair! I didn't even get a chance to tell her what happened!* There must be a million kids all over the world who really *did* sneak out last night, but I didn't and here I am getting blamed for something I absolutely did not do!

"Stop crying!" my mother screams. This is when I notice that she's crying, too.

We both cry all the way to my father's house. Not a word is spoken until she puts the car in park. Then she blows out a lungful of air and says matter-of-factly, "Karis, you might want to talk to your father about taking some precautions."

"Mom!"

She gives me the hand. "It's one thing to mess up *your* life; it's another thing to bring an innocent child into your mess."

I squeeze my eyes and cry, "But I'm not *doing* anything! That's what I've been trying to tell you!"

When I open my eyes, my mom has her back to her door's panel and she's staring at me. "Humor me, Karis. What happened? Why were you climbing into the window this morning wearing the same clothes you had on last night, hair a mess, eyes looking like you haven't slept a wink? Explain it."

I throw my head back on the headrest and look toward the roof of my mom's car. I might as well tell the truth, the whole truth, and nothing but the truth because at this point, I'm already in over my head. What difference does it make if I drown in ten feet of water or fifty? Let's get it on. "I had to get the ring," I stated.

"Where was the ring?"

"Outside on the ground."

She fires, "Why was it outside on the ground?"

"Because I dropped it when I was climbing back into the window the night before last."

"Why were you climbing back into the window the night before last?"

I admit, "Because I climbed out of the window to go talk to Javon in his car."

"I've heard enough." She ends the discussion, gets out of the car, and slams the door before I have a chance to say another word.

chapter twenty-four

When my dad opens the door, I put the ring in his hand and go straight to my room with two of the trash bags. My mother brings in the last one, drops it on the floor, and walks out of his house. She doesn't even say good-bye.

I close the door to my room, crumple onto my bed, and cry so hard that my body starts to shake all over. I really can't tell what hurts more—my mom, Javon, or my dad. Plus I don't have a car and I only have about half my clothes. Everything hurts, and it's all compounded by the fact that Javon was never worth it. Neither was Derrick or anything else. And now my mom has kicked me out of the house. I'm going to have a long, boring life at my dad's house with his crazy new wife. I can't believe this!

I search through my bags and find my journal. This day has got to be recorded.

Dear Me,

I haven't cried this much in a long time. I can't remember EVER crying so hard for so many different reasons. I've gotta get myself together. This ain't me—three trash bags full of clothes, living at my daddy's house, estranged from my mom. No, she and I don't get along, but it's never been like this.

What hurts more than anything is that when I really wanted to tell the truth about the ring and Javon, my mom wouldn't hear it. So much for integrity.

Today goes down in history as the worst day of my life. Seriously. Nothing else compares.

Karis Crying-Like-a-Baby Reed

To verify the claim that today holds the "Worst Day" record, I flip back through the pages of my journal and read through this year of my life. A funny thing happens. I'm reading through all this stuff I've done since, like, August, and I'm amazed at myself. Skipping school, detentions, lying about having homework and projects so I wouldn't have to go to church, forging my mom's name on a bad progress report, going to Derrick's, the cell phone incident. Not to mention the stuff I *haven't* written. If somebody had told me a year ago that this would be *my* journal, I wouldn't have believed them. I would have said, "I'm not that stupid," or "I have more respect for myself than to do those things" because the bottom line is: I know better.

I guess I can't blame my mom for kicking me out. *I'm* the one who's been straight trippin' lately. I'm wondering what my journal will say this time next year, and it scares me. What else might I live to regret if I keep down this path?

The stench from my armpits finds its way to my nose.

I need a shower. As I search through my bags for clothes and fresh undergarments, I'm realizing all the stuff I left at my mom's. I didn't remember to get anything from the bathroom—toiletries, curling irons, hair gel, girly products, makeup. Nothing.

I'll have to use what I can find for now. Fortunately, my dad uses aerosol deodorant. I'll smell like a grown man, but I suppose that's better than smelling like funk. He uses store-brand lotion, so I'll probably have to come back in an hour and reapply. I'm also noticing for the first time that his towels are scratchy. He doesn't even have fabric softener here! My dad needs help, but I am not the one. I wonder where Shereese is. I'm not going to ask about her, though, because he'll start talking about the ring.

My dad waits until around twelve to knock on my door. "Karis?"

"Yes."

"Come on out and join me for lunch."

"Why?" I whine.

"It is Christmas Day, Karis."

"Doesn't feel like it."

Gently, he turns the knob on the door and pokes his head into the room. "We need to talk. If you're going to be living with me, we're gonna have to lay down some rules."

I follow him back to the kitchen, dragging my feet the whole way. I have no idea what rules my dad will come up with. I'm sure I can find a way around them, whatever they are. The only question is: am I up to it?

My dad sets a place for me at the table. I fold my arms around my waist and lay my face down on the cold plate. He walks toward me with a salad bowl in one hand, tongs in the other. "Are you going to lift your head so I can put food on your plate?"

"I'm not hungry."

He steps over to his plate and mumbles, "Did you get drunk last night?"

"No," I murmur.

"Sure looks like it."

"Mmmm," I mumble.

"I remember the first time I got drunk," he recalls as he stuffs his face with salad and spaghetti. "Me, Donnie, and Fredrick drank all night one time. I couldn't stand the smell of food for days! Karis, drinking is serious business. Donnie died in a car wreck that next year. Drunk driving. I am not going to get you a car if you start drinking and doing drugs."

"I'm not doing drugs, Daddy," I moan into the plate.

"Well, I was wondering if you took the ring because you needed the money to buy—"

A little louder this time. "I'm not drinking or doing drugs, nor am I stealing so that I can drink or do drugs."

He cocks his head to one side and warns, "All right," in that I'm-watching-you tone. Now I can safely add alcohol and illegal substances to the list of things I've been falsely accused of doing.

The day drags on. My life is so crazy, I decide the best thing I can do is escape to another world. I finish reading *Things Fall Apart* and realize that I'm going to have to read the last four or five chapters again, because I don't really get it. Or maybe I'll just get the SparkNotes online.

Later, as I prepare to go to bed, I'm wondering if my mom is going to call me. It occurs to me that I could call her, but I really don't know what to say. Today is the maddest I've ever seen my mom. She might not even speak to me if I call her. I don't think I could take any more rejection today, so I abandon the idea of contacting my mom.

If I can't talk to my mom, I don't want to talk to anyone right now. It's only eight o'clock, but since I have no life, I might as well go to sleep. I slide between the sheets and wait for sleep to come, but sleep is nowhere near this bedroom. All I can do is replay this morning over and over again in my head. My mom's face was so unforgettably painted with anguish. It's like for the past sixteen years, she's been dreading the moment I would let her down, and I finally made it happen today.

Maybe there's such a thing as the mom-fulfilling prophecy thing—where the thing that your mom always believed about you finally comes true. I mean, really, since I got to be about ten years old, all she's done is tell me that I had better not get all wild and crazy when I become a teenager. Why would she need to keep telling me those things if, deep down in her heart, she didn't believe that I had it in me to *be* wild and crazy?

And I know she's always trying to replay her mistakes to keep me from repeating them, but every time she tells me that having a baby at sixteen makes life miserable, I feel like she's reminding me that I was/am the big "oops" in her life. I'm the reason she didn't get to go to college right away, I'm the reason she owes thousands of dollars in student loans, which is why she can't get the car she really wants, which is why we can't move to a bigger house, et cetera to infinity. I'm also the reason she doesn't date. I've heard her tell my grandmother that she doesn't want to bring all kinds of men around me and set a bad example.

Well, I'd rather her move on with her life and set a bad example (like my dad) than keep bringing up the fact that my very existence has been nothing but a burden to her. Maybe she's been waiting for this moment all my life—the moment she could get rid of me and pick up where her freedom left off.

Just when I think I'm completely out of tears, my eyes amaze me by producing a fresh batch. When I sit down and really think about things, it's easy to arrive at these negative thoughts.

And yet, in my heart, I don't think all of that is true. Maybe a tiny bit of it, but not all of it. My mom loves me. No matter how I got here or when I got here, I know she still loves me. Right?

Besides, she's always talking about how God has a big plan for me. He wouldn't have this big plan for me if He didn't want me here, right? Thinking of God makes me want to talk to Him. I have so many questions running through my mind right now. I need to do something that I know is constant; something that always makes me feel better.

I get out of bed and let my body slump down to praying position. It's too cold in this house right now, so I pull the comforter off the bed and wrap myself in it. I may be down here for a while.

"God, I'm sorry for everything. Please forgive me. I know my mom is mad at me right now. Both my parents are mad at me, and they think the worst. You and I know the truth, and I guess that is what matters most. I ask that You would touch their hearts so they'll listen to me, even though I've lied a lot lately.

"I also want You to show me that . . . I'm . . . supposed to be here. I know You made me and You gave me life. But how can a good thing like my life come from something as wrong as two teenagers having a baby? I know, in my heart, that I'm a great person. I love You, I love my parents. I'm just having a moment right now, Lord, and I need You. In Jesus' name I pray, Amen."

When I stop praying, I don't want to open my eyes, so I sit there with them closed for a while as tears worm down my face. The comforter completely envelops me, creating a pocket of warmth. I sit here still feeling God, and I imagine Him hugging me right now. I think about it so long, it almost feels like if I open my eyes, I'll see Him here. My grandmother has a black-and-white-striped shawl, which she calls her "prayer shawl." The last time she was here, I saw her wrapped up in the shawl, praying in the living room in the early hours of the morning. I thought she was just doing it because she liked the shawl. Now I understand.

My mom doesn't call until the day after Christmas. She talks to my dad for about ten minutes and then tells my dad to put me on the phone. I know she's going to fuss at me, but I can't tell you how happy I am that she actually wants to speak to me.

"Karis?" Her voice is dull and muffled. She's been crying just like me.

"Yes, ma'am."

"I've prayed and I've talked to your daddy, and we've made a decision."

In the few seconds I have to think, I imagine everything she could say: she's kicking me out for good; I've got to go to private school; they're sending me for a mental evaluation; they're sending me away to boot camp; or I'm going to be a ward of the state. How has my life come to this? Everything I ever dreamed about—gone. Just like that.

My mom sentences me. "I'm going to . . ." She sniffles. "I'm going to step away from women's ministry for a while and concentrate more on raising you."

All the blood drains from my face, because this is worse than I thought. Instead of making *me* give up *my* life, my mom is willing to sacrifice *hers*. *Step away from women's ministry?* I can't believe it. How could she? When she's up on stage speaking, it's like God Himself is talking to the people. And when she prays with the women who come to the altar, I can tell she's doing something special. They walk down the aisle one way, and get up with fresh hope in their tear-filled eyes. People love her. People get to know God because of her. She can't give it up. "But, Momma, you *love* helping people."

"What kind of mother would I be if I help everyone except my own daughter?"

"You're a great mother. It's not your fault. I . . . it's *me*. I'm the problem, okay? I've been the *big* problem in your life for sixteen years."

My mom gasps. "Is that what you think, Karis?"

I can't turn off the waterworks. Between sobs, I answer her. "Last night, I was thinking . . . if you and daddy could live your lives all over again, I wouldn't even be here. Then we wouldn't have all these problems—you could live your life, daddy could live his life, and everyone would be happier if you two hadn't made a mistake—I mean, *me*—when you were teenagers."

I can tell my mom is crying as she manages the question, "Karis, I am so sorry if I made you feel this way. Is this why you've been acting out so much lately?"

"No, ma'am." The old me would have used this guilt card

to the fullest, but I just can't do it anymore. "This is just something I was thinking about last night."

She takes a few sniffles and says, "Karis, I want you to know that those thoughts were not of God, okay? The Bible is filled with stories of people whose parents weren't doing the right thing, but the children were still blessed by God. You remember the story of David and Bathsheba, right?"

"Yes," I say.

"David was altogether wrong for having Bathsheba's husband killed. And yet his son, Solomon, was the wisest man on earth. It is true that your daddy and I should not have been sexually active when I got pregnant with you. But I want you to know that God can take our mistakes and make them into something beautiful—like you. Sometimes we don't make the right decision, but if we turn it over to God, *He* can make the decision right.

"Karis, having you taught me the true meaning of Romans 8:28. All things really *do* work out for the good of them that love the Lord; the good, the bad, and the ugly can be used for His glory—in spite of our faults."

I interrupt her. "What if I hadn't been born, though? I mean, if you could make a different choice, you would, wouldn't you?"

My mom laughs slightly. "I think everyone who has walked the planet has something they would do differently if it were possible. I'm sure Adam and Eve would do things differently if they could do it over again. Then sin wouldn't have entered the world. But God didn't rewind time and allow them to do it again, no matter how devastating the ramifications. Instead, He arranged for a plan of redemption through His son, Jesus. I don't know what the world would have been like without

Adam and Eve's sin in the garden of Eden, but I'm glad to know Jesus now. The burden of sin has been lifted because God's grace, love, and mercy provided a path back to His very heart through Christ. That's what matters right now, Karis. I want you to always remember this, okay?"

The tears have stopped flowing. My mom has this no-nonsense way of explaining things when it comes to God, Jesus, and the Bible. I've seen her talk to women who looked like they were so beat down, they were about to faint. Then my mom starts praying for and with them, whispering things into their ears, quoting the Scriptures, and encouraging them until they get filled with new hope. I wish I could take back all the things I've done so she wouldn't feel the need to stop ministering to other women.

"Sweetheart, do you have your Bible with you?"

I'm thinking of all the things I stuffed into my backpack. I remember packing my Bible, but I don't know where it is at the moment. "I think so."

"Well, I've got to get back to work, but I want you to look in your concordance and look up the story of David and Bathsheba so you can read it again. David did some pretty horrible things that I'm sure he wished he could take back. He paid a price for his sins, but God forgave him, and David's son, Solomon, became the wisest man on earth despite the circumstances of his parents' union."

I remember reading about David in my Sunday school lessons. He is one of my favorite people in the Bible. Too bad I haven't spent much time thinking about David or anyone else who might inspire me to do the right thing. Lately, I haven't been thinking of anyone but myself.

My mom gets back to business with me. "Well, with the

help of the Lord, I am going to get you straightened out, Karis."

"I'm sorry, Momma."

"Is that all you have to say? Sorry?" Any other time, my mom might have said this sarcastically. Today, she's telling me what's on her mind, no yelling attached. We're two people having a medium-volume conversation.

"What can I say other than sorry?"

"You can say, 'I won't disobey again.' "

I reply honestly, "I can't say that because maybe I'd be lying."

"What makes you think you can't stop yourself from lying?"

"Because I'm always in trouble."

"Maybe you're always in trouble because you refuse to stay within the boundaries I set for you. Here's a novel idea, Karis: stay within the boundaries. I don't make boundaries and rules for my good health, I make them for *your* good. If you do what you're supposed to do, you wouldn't get in trouble and you wouldn't have to lie and disobey your way into even more trouble."

I think she's serious. She actually thinks that I can live within her boundaries. "Mom, nobody follows *all* the rules. I mean, isn't that what America is all about? If everybody followed the rules, no one would ever get rich or invent anything or do anything new. You gotta be your own person, make your own rules."

"Says who?"

"Says . . . the *whole world*."

My mother laughs at me. At first, it's soft. Then she's roaring in laughter. "Oh, Karis, you are something else."

"What's so funny?"

She calms herself down. "You know this is a lifelong battle that every person faces? Doing what you *know* is right versus doing what the *world* says is right or even what *feels* right. You're not the first person with this issue—it's all through the Bible. Abraham, the Israelites, Paul, and now Karis Reed."

I'm wondering aloud, "So *you* have this problem, too?"

"Of course."

"What do *you* do?"

I just know her answer is going to be something unreasonable. Something only grown-ups with boring lives would do. It's probably easy to do the right thing when you don't have the wrong thing staring you in the face. Really, when you're an average, regular adult and there's no school, no homework, and no one telling you what to do, how can you go wrong?

"I ask God to help me make decisions with integrity."

"But what kind of decisions do you have to make, Mom? You just . . . go to work, go to church, and come home. What kinds of stuff do you have to stay away from?" I plead my case.

"You think I'm not tempted to sin?" she asks.

"Well, I mean . . . no. Yeah. I guess you get tempted, I don't know." I'm trying to avoid telling her that she doesn't have a life, but I don't think it's working.

She rattles off a list of her issues. "I have men approaching me and suggesting ungodly things, I have patients who curse at me, I have a supervisor who is often unreasonable, and every month when I sit down to do bills I am tempted to make money doing things outside of God's call on my life. How's that for temptation to sin?"

Okay, that first thing was kinda nasty, but I suppose the

rest are legitimate. "So you just use integrity to help you make decisions?"

"Yes. And what I forgot to tell you the other night is that integrity isn't only about telling the truth after you've made a decision. It's about respecting yourself and loving people enough to tell them the truth. And if you claim to be trying to live with integrity, stay true to the *real* you by making decisions that line up with who you *really* are."

While we're having this open, honest discussion, I've worked up enough nerve to come clean. It bothers me that my mom thinks I'm so bad. "Momma, I'm gonna tell you something with lots of integrity. You ready?"

She takes a deep breath. "Yes."

"Please don't interrupt me, okay?"

"Okay."

Here is my chance. I close my eyes and say everything without taking a breath because I don't want my mom to mix me up with a bunch of questions. "Okay. I did not sneak out last night. I snuck out the night before last so I could be with Javon, but we did not go anywhere. We were sitting outside the whole time in his car. We did not do anything except kiss. Well, he did try to get with me, but I told him no and anyway I don't like him anymore because even though he is cute, he is rude, he steals, he's crazy, and he has no integrity."

I'm waiting for her to reach through this phone and pop me. Instead, she says, "I believe you."

I know I'm still grounded, I know she's still mad at me, and there is the very real possibility that everything I just told her will be used against me in the near future. But I have to say, those were the best three words I'd heard from my mom in a long time.

chapter twenty-five

I'm staying at my dad's house through the rest of the Christmas break. I did what my mom said by asking God to help me, because, since I'm out of school while grounded *with* integrity, I have to stay off the phone with my friends in order to follow the rules. Well, He must have heard my prayer, because Tamisha has gone to Michigan to spend the holidays with her family (not that she would talk to me anyway), Sydney is in a basketball tournament, and my dad took a few days off work, so he's here most of the time. It also helps that I happen to be single right now.

My dad and I have just been hanging out together these last few days of the year. We've popped popcorn and we're watching an old Wesley Snipes movie when I finally work up the nerve to ask him about Shereese.

He sticks out his lips and shakes his head.

"Come on, tell me," I prod.

"It's over between me and Shereese."

I'm happy for me, but I'm sad for him. I think my dad really liked her. I liked her, too, until I saw her true colors. "I'm sorry I ruined your love life."

"No, you didn't ruin it," he disagrees as he puts an arm around me on the couch. "When she opened up that box and saw the cereal, she flipped. I mean, she really flipped. She called you and your momma everything but a child of God and she cussed me out like a drunken sailor. I realized then that I was already having enough trouble with one little girl. I didn't need two problem children on my hands."

I raise up and look at him, declaring, "I'm not a problem child!"

"Well, lately you've been *acting* like one."

I am offended. I have been acting *great* since I had that talk with my mom yesterday. How far back does "lately" have to go before we can safely call it "the past"? "I'm all better now, Daddy."

He nods. "Good. For a minute there, I thought I was going to have to break out my brown leather belt and give you one of those good old-fashioned country whippins'."

I smack my lips in response. He raises an eyebrow and warns me, "My momma used to tell me: you're never too old for a whippin'. As long as you keep actin' up, you are more than eligible for a beat-down."

I lay my head back down on his arm. "I'm sorry for everything, okay? But don't worry. You'll get the right girlfriend."

"Are you going to help me pick her out this time?"

"Oh!" I pop up from the sofa and begin trying to sell him on someone I'd had in mind for him. "My computer teacher—

she's cute, for real, Daddy. She's, like, my height, a little lighter than me, she's got long, black hair, and she dresses real nice. And she's smart, too! She knows, like, everything about computers."

"I am not dating one of your teachers," he protests.

I nod my head and wink at him. "Come to parent night at school. It'll change your mind. But wait 'til May, 'cause if you mess up, she might give me an F."

He laughs at me. "I wonder about you sometimes, Karis. I really do."

"Hey, I'm just tellin' the truth! People can be crazy."

"I'm glad you realize that." My dad's tone is more serious now. He nudges my head off his shoulder and forces me to look at him. "The boy you were talking to—what was his name?"

I play dumb for a moment, squinting my eyes and shaking my head.

"Jaimon? Jamal? You know who I'm talking about."

I give. "Javon."

"As I understand it, you snuck out of the house to be with him?"

"Yes," I admit, but I need to qualify this. "We didn't go anywhere, Daddy, I promise. We were just sitting in the car."

This conversation feels awkward. I cannot talk to my dad about boys. He thinks all boys are the same. He also thinks I'm silly enough to believe everything they say. Okay, so I listened to Derrick and Javon, but I'm smarter now. I have learned my lesson.

He continues, "Sitting in the car leads to kissing in the car, and kissing in the car . . ."

I throw my hands over my ears. If my dad says the word

sex, I will die. "All right, Daddy, I hear you. You don't have to go on and on about it."

"All right, Karis. I'm not trying to become a grandfather before my time," he admonishes me.

The phone rings and my dad reaches past me to answer it. "Hello? Oh, you serious? Man . . . how bad? Oh, good . . . okay, we'll be right there." He hangs up and gives me a somber expression.

"What?"

"That was your mom on the phone. Your friend Sydney is at her hospital. Sydney was injured today in the basketball tournament. She's going to be okay, but she could use a friend right now."

I rush to my bedroom and grab my purse. On the way to the hospital, my problems get smaller and smaller. Here I am worried about the next couple of months, and Sydney's problem could affect the rest of her life. All the hard work, all the hours of practice, all the blood, sweat, and tears gone down the drain on one play. She wasn't even doing the wrong thing like me. She was doing the right thing and got hurt. It doesn't seem fair.

My dad calls my mom when we get to the parking lot. She meets us at the west entrance and leads us to Sydney. As we ride up the elevator, my mom explains that Sydney was diving for a loose ball and collided with another player. Sydney wasn't able to move her arms or her legs, so they rushed her to my mom's hospital. X-rays, spine, and nerve tests show that her neck is not broken—only sprained. She should be fine, but they have to observe her until she regains sensation and use of her limbs.

"Is she really gonna be okay, Momma?" I ask. "Tell me the truth."

"Yes. She will. But, honey, when you've lost the ability to move your body, it's the scariest thing on earth. And you need people next to you, supporting you. Sydney's mom asked me to call you."

We talked all the way up to Sydney's room. I'm the first to go in. It's like another world. A dark, quiet, suspended world. I've never been in this world before, and I don't ever want to go again. But Sydney's here and she has asked me to join her here, so I have no choice.

Mrs. Norman is sitting on a chair beside Sydney, holding her hand. Mr. Norman is asleep upright in another chair on the other side of Sydney, and Angelique is conked out on a cot near the foot of the bed.

When Mrs. Norman sees me, she runs toward me and sinks into a hug. I feel her body weight. I feel her sadness flow through me, warm and heavy. "Karis, thank you for coming. Sydney said she wanted you here to pray with her."

"She wants *me* to pray?"

"Yes. She wants *you* to pray." Mrs. Norman walks back to wake her family members. I hear her whisper to Sydney, "Honey, open your eyes. Karis is here. Let's pray."

I look over at my mom, and she gives me a nod of confidence.

Slowly, I walk to Sydney's bedside. She looks up at me and a tear rolls from her eye, disappearing into the braids that Tamisha put in. "Thanks for coming. You're the one who always tries to make everything right with God."

I nod, letting the truth of her words sink into my heart. All this time, I thought Sydney was hating on me for the things I say about Jesus, God, and church. I guess she was just watching me to see if I meant it.

Sydney's mother takes a tissue and wipes Sydney's eyes and nose for her. Sydney looks me in the eye and cries, "I can't move anything, Karis. I'm scared."

"You're gonna be okay. God is here," I assure her. My dad walks into the room. Now my parents and her family start to circle the bed. "Let's pray," I say. We're all grabbing hands now. I hold out my hand for Sydney, and when her hand doesn't move, it hits me: she can't even raise her hand. I don't know what I was thinking. I take a deep breath and lift Sydney's hand into mine.

"Father God, we're standing here . . . around this hospital bed . . . with Sydney. Sydney Norman. We want to thank You for watching over her tonight as she played basketball. We thank You that the doctors say everything will be okay. We thank You because even when things look bad, You are still in control. You're always watching over us, even when we don't do such a good job ourselves. Now, Father, we're asking for a quick recovery. Give Sydney the strength she needs to continue to play basketball and . . . fulfill every purpose that You have for her life. And, Father, thank You for letting Sydney come to know You as a healer, as a source of peace, and the God of her life, too. In Jesus' name we pray, Amen."

There must be twenty "Amens" in here. I look up and see that the whole basketball team crowded into the room as I was praying. Half of them are crying, and the other half look dazed.

As they start taking turns talking to Sydney, I push back toward my parents. "Cool prayer, Karis," one of the basketball team members says to me.

I don't really know how to respond, so I just smile.

Mrs. Norman catches me by the arm. She's drying her face

as she tells me, "You know, I listen to you girls talking and laughing all the time, and I couldn't figure out for the life of me why Sydney wanted you to be the first to pray for her. Now I understand why it had to be you."

I smile and say, "Thank you," but honestly, *I* don't see why.

My parents and I ride back downstairs on the elevator. For some reason, my mom can't stop crying. She's not breaking down or anything. Just a tear every few seconds. When we get back to the west doors, my dad tells us to wait while he goes to get the car. My mom and I are standing between the two sets of sliding glass doors when she reaches over and hugs my neck. "Karis, I'm so proud of you."

"Momma, I can't breathe," I manage to say.

She leans back. "Let me get a good look at you."

"What?"

"I saw something tonight that God promised me many years ago. Everything, even the disobedient choices we make, can be turned around for good. What I saw God do through you tonight was . . . amazing."

I don't get it. "You sound like Sydney's mom."

"Sydney's mom was right," my mother confirms. "There *is* something special about you, and everything I do, every rule I make, every time I fuss—it's all because I want to protect and nurture that something and see it flourish in your life. That's all I want for you, Karis. God's best."

My mom does her motherly thing, pulling the hood over my head before I go out into the cold.

"How do you know all this about me?"

Another tear falls from her face down her cheek, and then she puts her forehead squarely on top of mine. "Because, Karis, it's in your natural and spiritual blood."

chapter twenty-six

Thank God my mom decided to let me move back home. I'm sad that she rejected a few of her speaking offers and turned down some overtime opportunities at the hospital, but if I'm totally honest with myself, I have to admit: I will be glad to be able to spend more time with her. Is that selfish? I hope not. I don't want to spend more time with my mom *forever*—just until I can prove to her that I'm not this prodigal daughter.

Last night, we went to see a movie together. Granted, no guys approached me because I was with her, but it was okay. We went out to eat afterwards. My mom and I shared a jumbo-sized order of catfish and fries. We were so stuffed that we could hardly scoot ourselves out of the booth.

"Karis, you want to drive home?" she asked as we were leaving the restaurant. I turned to face her and make sure I'd heard her correctly. My face said *huh*? So she repeated herself. "Do you want to drive home?"

I'm sure my eyes must have been saucers. "Yes, ma'am!" My mom knows I have a driver's license, but she has never actually seen me behind the wheel. I did all my driving practice with my dad over the holidays.

She fished through her purse, then gave me the keys. I was never so intimidated in my life. One false move and she could have banned me from driving her car forever, which is approximately how long it will take before I get my car in the spring. My mom was trying really hard to appear relaxed, but the death grip she had on the door's handle gave her away as I put the car in reverse and relinquished our parking spot.

"Are you sure you can handle this?" I asked her.

She was almost hyperventilating. "Yeah, yeah. There's a first time for almost everything."

I drove home as safely as possible. About halfway there, my mom took her hand off the handle and gave me a compliment. "You're doing a really good job, Karis."

I looked over at her to say thanks, but before I could get a word out, she pointed and barked, "Keep your eyes on the road."

We made it home in four pieces—me, my mom, the car, and her jumbled nerves.

School resumes tomorrow. I still haven't talked to Tamisha about the situation with Marlon. Actually, there is no situation with Marlon. I haven't written him back yet and, at this point, I'm almost too embarrassed to let him know that I couldn't write him back because I didn't know what to say.

If I write him back now, he'll think I'm not a reliable person. If I never write him back, he'll think I don't care, which will probably make Tamisha even more angry with me. I am clueless about what to do.

I know Sydney has enough to worry about with her recovery, but I've got to do something before I walk into school tomorrow. I don't want a bunch of evil glares to transpire between Tamisha and me. The only person who might have a clue about what to do is our mutual friend.

I'm still grounded, so I'm not supposed to be on the phone. This is an emergency, however, and I can't think of any other way to get the situation resolved without breaking this one cardinal rule of grounding. My mom is in her room, probably reading. Back in the old days, I would have just made the sneak. Not anymore. It's been a good week with my mom, and I don't want to ruin this.

Against my better judgment, I make the trek to her room and prepare to ask her if I can use the phone. On the way to her bedroom, I pass the mirror in the hallway and catch a glimpse of myself. Could this be Responsible Karis Reed staring back at me? *Ha!* I laugh at myself, wondering if I'll still be smiling when I walk past this mirror again.

I knock on my mom's door. She gives me the word and I enter. "What's up?"

"Nothing much," I say, plopping down on her bed in a helpless fashion. I am completely at her mercy, and I don't like it. But what else can I do? I must approach this carefully. I glance down and quickly read the title of the book she's reading—*Praying for Real*. "Whatcha reading?"

"Oh, it's just a book on practical prayer and how to stay in a spirit of prayer throughout the day."

"You want to pray all day?" I'm wondering out loud.

She laughs a bit and answers, "I want to stay in a spirit of prayer all day—just talking to the Lord, thanking Him, hearing from Him so that I'll know how to handle life's little issues."

I wish I could find out what God wants me to do about Marlon and Tamisha. The whole thing is just messed up, but I can't see any way for God to fix it since I have so thoroughly complicated things by evading them both.

Breathing deeply, I get back to my mission. "Well, Mom, I need to ask you a question. And if you need to pray about it, that's okay, but I hope you get an answer really soon. Like in maybe five minutes."

She squints her eyes, lays the book against her chest, and nods for me to continue.

"I really, really, really need to talk to Sydney and probably Tamisha tonight."

She nods again. I had not expected to be giving details, but apparently that's what she wants. "We have a little situation."

My mom raises an eyebrow and cocks her head to one side.

"No! No! It's not a bad situation, Mom, it's just a . . . friend type of an issue."

Her head is right side up again, face softening. "Is there anything I can help you with?"

This is interesting. My mom helps women solve problems all the time. I suppose that's the key word, though—*women*. This is a young lady problem. "No. I can handle it myself."

"Well, if it's that important, I suppose you can talk to them. Briefly. Ten minutes, Karis, that's it."

I bound toward her and plant the biggest kiss on her cheek. She's totally shocked. Come to think of it, I'm rather shocked myself. I haven't kissed my mom in a long time, but God knows it was kinda cool for some strange reason. When I was little, I used to sit on my mom's foot and hug her leg while she walked around with me hanging on to her for dear life. Those were the good ole days.

"Good night, Mom."

"Night, Karis."

I walk past that mirror again and wink at myself. I suppose I am pretty responsible these days.

I pick up the phone and dial.

"Hey, Sydney. You ready for school tomorrow?"

Sydney takes a deep breath. "As ready as I can be, I guess. The doctor says I need to take it slow and easy. I'm going to get a special pass to leave every class five minutes early for the next couple of weeks."

"Oh, good. Have you had any more headaches?"

"No, thank God. Those stopped a few days ago."

Did she just say "Thank God"? Let me agree with her right away. "Yeah, thank God."

Sydney beats me to the punch. "Have you talked to Tamisha yet?"

"No. Have you?"

"Uh, yeah."

"What did she say about me and Marlon?" I ask.

"She says she doesn't want her brother to be played."

"Well, did you tell her that I would never do a thing like that?"

"No," Sydney says. "I told her that *you* don't *have* enough game to play Marlon."

"Ha, ha. Very funny, Sydney."

"Well, you asked. I answered."

"That was *not* the correct response," I assure her.

Sydney sighs. "You need to talk to her yourself and straighten this whole thing out. If you like Marlon, go for it. Marlon put the *F* in *fine,* okay? I ain't mad atcha. Tamisha will just have to get over it. And *you* will have to stop trying to be a playgirl."

"Who says I'm a playgirl?"

"Javon, Quinten, Derrick . . . need I say more?"

I'm shocked at that middle name. "Quinten? Who said I was with Quinten?"

"I've seen you two flirting. Quinten has a thing for you, Karis—for real."

"You think so?" I ask.

"See! That's what I'm talking about. If you're gonna go for Marlon, you'll have to stop with all these locals for Tamisha's sake. You can't cheat on someone who's away fighting in a war."

I practice pleading my case to Sydney. "But it's not like Marlon and I would be engaged or anything. Nothing serious could go down between me and him while he's away. We'd just be forming the friendship for something that *might* happen later. You know?"

"Nope," Sydney disagrees with me. "You cannot let his family see you talking to other guys. If you wanna start this thing with Marlon, it's got to be Marlon all the way, or his family will feel disrespected. You gotta understand that, Karis."

"That's stupid."

"That's politics. So, did you write him back already? What did he say?"

I admit, "I haven't written him back yet."

"What! What kind of soldier support is that?"

"I don't know what to say, Sydney."

"For the sake of the United States of America, I am going to hang up this phone right now so you can go write Marlon back. You cannot leave his heart hanging like this, Karis, it's not right. It's unpatriotic. Bye." Sydney hangs up on me before I have the chance to talk this out with her.

No matter. She doesn't see things my way anyway. What is my way, by the way? No wonder she doesn't see my way—it doesn't exist. This whole thing is crazy. I've gotta talk to Tamisha. What's the worst thing that could happen? I suppose she could stop speaking to me. She could decide that her brother is too good for me and start hating me. Then, when I marry Marlon, she'd be my evil sister-in-law. She'd snub her nose at me, but I know Tamisha. Somehow she would still manage to treat my kids, her nieces and nephews, well. What about the holidays? I don't want to see my ex-friend who hates my guts but loves my kids every year. This is crazy!

I pick up the phone to call Tamisha and then quickly change my mind before it connects. I have no idea what to say to her. My next best bet is to reply to Marlon's letter. Pen and paper in hand, nothing in mind, I try again to write. This feels like a standardized writing exam. Mrs. Clawson always tells us to review the prompt and brainstorm ideas when we get stuck. If it works on an English test, maybe it'll work now.

Marlon's letter is before my face again for the umpteenth time. I'm searching for an "in" or some kind of angle to take. I'm so deep into his letter that my mom's knock on my door startles me.

"You off the phone yet?" she wants to know as she peeks her head into my room.

"Oh, yes, ma'am," I respond, folding Marlon's note.

My mom takes the liberty of stepping into my room. "Everything okay between you girls?"

I put my hands over my face and let out an exhausted groan. "No. But it will be as soon as I figure out what to do."

"Have you prayed about it?"

This feels like one of those cheesy after-school movies where the music starts playing as the mother comes over, caresses the daughter, and solves all the daughter's problems with a five-minute monologue-slash-1960s flashback. I can't go out like that. My mom is semi-cool, but I don't think I want her in all my business. "No. It's not that serious," I say.

"It doesn't have to be a life-or-death situation in order for you to pray about it, Karis. Just give it a try. You'd be surprised how much God cares about every little thing in your life," she states as she stays her distance. "He'll give you the integrity to make the right decisions. Good night."

Just like that, she leaves me alone to think about whether or not I should pray about this whole Marlon thing. Despite how stupid I feel, I close my eyes, clasp my hands beneath my chin, and pray, "God, even though I don't really think You deal with stuff like boyfriends and girlfriends, I'm just going to ask you this one thing, because this is not just about me. It's also about Tamisha. And it's also about war and stuff, so I think You might want to get involved. Please show me what to do about Marlon. In Jesus' name, Amen."

Maybe I was expecting to see something fall from the sky, I don't know, but when I open my eyes, I feel no closer to an answer than I was five minutes ago. I take my mom's advice and decide there's nothing else I can do about this situation until I get to school tomorrow. Or until I hear from God, whichever comes first.

chapter twenty-seven

I'm sitting in social studies class listening to Mr. Whitley talk about Shakespeare. Shouldn't we be having this discussion in English class? Well, I can wait. I'm in no rush to talk to Tamisha—or *not* talk to her. This morning, I didn't call to ask her to pick me up, and she didn't offer. I hate not knowing what to do.

"Karis!" Mr. Whitley interrupts my train of thought.

I snap back into reality. "Yes?"

"What do you think it means?"

"What means?"

"Shakespeare's quote—'to thine own self be true?'"

All sixty eyes in the classroom are on me as I ponder the question in terror. Stalling, I say out loud, "To thine own self . . . be true?"

Jacob Stanley, our class clown, jokes, "That's what he

just said." The room snickers, and I know I have to speak up.

"It means that you have to be honest with yourself; know what you feel deep down inside and be true to it," I think myself into an answer.

"Very good, Miss Reed," Mr. Whitley relents, probably disappointed that he didn't get to nail me with this one. He goes on to his next intended victim.

Wait a minute—this is the answer I've been looking for all day! All week! Since I got the letter from Marlon! I have to be true to myself first, and the truth is: I can't go there with him. It feels too weird and goofy, plus it puts me in an awkward position with Tamisha. I pull the letter from Marlon out of my purse. I suppose I've been carrying it around in hopes that I could hold it under ultraviolet light, maybe, and discover a clue about how to reply. Now I know.

Thank You, God!

Dear Me,

What a Christmas season! Okay, I didn't get my car, my heart got broken, and I am still somewhat on punishment for all the stuff that went down with Javon. I still must look at the bright side: my mom and I are talking more, my dad is not going to marry Shereese, and I learned a big lesson about boys. DO NOT MAKE EXCUSES FOR THEM SO THAT YOU CAN KEEP DATING THEM! The next time somebody steals from their job and makes me steal gas, I am so through with him!

Sydney is getting better every day. She may be able to compete in the finals, if we make it to state. She has even come to church with me a few times—I think she actually has a crush on Henry! Can you believe that?

I've been praying a lot more and trying to walk in integrity lately. My mom got me a book about integrity and I try to read a chapter every night. No, I am not turning into my mother. It's just a good book, that's all.

My biggest thing: I told Marlon the truth about my feelings. I told him that I was flattered, but I couldn't ever be more than a "little sister" to him because it would be too awkward for the two of us, as well as for Tamisha. He said he understood—and he told me that he appreciated my honesty. He also said that he had a comrade who would love to meet someone new. Seriously, in like two weeks I got a letter from the guy! His name is Lamar Brooks. He's eighteen and he's from Chicago. Since writing is the only thing I can do for the next I-don't-know-how-many weeks or months, I have written Lamar three times already. He has written me twice—with a picture. So far so good on the boyfriend quiz! He says that if he makes it out of the war alive, the first thing he'll do is fly to Texas and take me out. If I keep up with this integrity, I feel fairly certain that I won't be grounded when Lamar comes to sweep me off my feet.

Karis Trying-to-Live-with-Integrity Reed

Reading Group Guide

Introduction

Karis Reed doesn't *try* to get in trouble—but, sometimes, trouble gets in the way. An unauthorized trip to a male friend's house puts Karis at odds with her mother, a minister who is determined to make sure that Karis doesn't repeat her mistake of getting pregnant at sixteen. Against Karis's better judgment, she takes part in a plan to keep her social life flowing just beneath her mother's radar.

Enter a self-proclaimed bad boy, a trifling potential stepmother, a deployed soldier, and threats to relationships with two of Karis's best friends. When Karis's mother finds out about her deception she is fed up and decides that Karis may be better off living with her father. Feelings that Karis could never before articulate come to the surface when she realizes that there's nothing left to lose when you've lost your parents' trust. Through a renewed faith in God's plan for her life, Karis decides to recommit herself to living with integrity.

Discussion Questions

1. "Basically, she lost her teen years when she got pregnant with me at sixteen—but how it that *my* problem? Why do I have to pay for her mistakes? I'm not my mom, and she's

not me!" How does Karis's turning sixteen trigger a shift in her relationship with her mother? In what ways is Karis directly and indirectly responsible for this shift? Do you feel that Karis's mother is being overprotective?

2. Explain Karis's attraction to Javon. What does her decision to pursue a relationship with him on the sly, using a borrowed cell phone from a friend, reveal about her character? Based on the details he reveals to Karis about his life, how moral of a person is Javon? Why doesn't Karis's mother object to their budding relationship?

3. "You can still be you and do what you're supposed to do. Actually, you can't fulfill your purpose *without* being the you that God created." How does Karis's mother's faith in her daughter guide her parenting? To what extent does Karis share her mother's religious beliefs?

4. How would you describe Karis's friendships with Sydney and Tamisha? When Karis accidentally incurs excessive cell phone charges using Sydney's sister's phone, why doesn't she immediately own up to her mistake? When Marlon contacts her from Iraq, why does Karis decide to conceal that from his sister, Tamisha? How does the resolution of these separate crises impact Karis's friendships with both girls?

5. "There's something about you, Karis. I don't know what it is, but you make me want to do the right thing." How would you assess Karis's moral instincts? What role do her parents play in her shaping these beliefs and attitudes? How does she convey her faith to her friends? What role does her diary

play in her establishing what it is that she believes? To what extent does her moral compass protect her from *really* getting into trouble?

6. What does the "Boyfriend Quiz" that Sydney, Tamisha, and Karis devise reveal about the nature of their feelings about the opposite sex? What is most important to them and why? How does their quiz reveal both their wisdom and their naïveté about romantic relationships? If you were to apply their quiz to someone you really care about, what kind of ranking would he or she receive?

7. "And since I'm the reason she *has* the ring, I can also be the reason she *doesn't* have the ring." Is Karis justified in taking the ring her father intends to use to propose to Shereese? Why does Shereese suspect Karis's interference is an attempt to bring her parents back together, and do you agree or disagree with that assessment?

8. What spurs Karis's mother's decision to have her daughter move out to go and live with her father? How does Karis feel about this change in her domestic arrangements? Why does her mother feel that it is a good time for them to live separately? To what extent does her abrupt solution to the difficulties involved in raising her daughter seem in keeping with her approach as a parent?

9. Of the many different moments of trouble that Karis finds herself in, which were the most memorable or compelling to you, and why? To what extent are the people Karis surrounds herself with responsible for the trouble that she encounters?

10. What does Karis's mother mean when she says she strives to live a life with integrity? How does living a life with integrity connect with living a life faithful to God's desires? How does Karis try to live with integrity in her own life? Can you identify an example from your experiences in which you have chosen a path of integrity?

A Conversation with Michelle Stimpson

Q: *Trouble in My Way* is your first young adult novel. What were some of the challenges you faced in writing a novel with a teenager as a protagonist?
A: **Actually, I found it pretty easy. I'm a big kid at heart, so falling into this character's mindset was like second nature.**

Q: To what extent did the process of writing *Trouble in My Way* take you back to your own hijinks as a teenager?
A: **Writing this book took me *way* back! I have kept a journal since I was twelve, so I have a record of the dramas and antics I experienced as a teen. Writing this book almost made me feel as though I was writing in one of my old journals.**

Q: How did you first come up with the idea for the story of *Trouble in My Way*?
A: **I didn't really come up with a story first. For this book, I came up with the main character first and then built the story around her. I knew I wanted to write about a girl who has a good heart but doesn't always do the right thing. Once I had a feel for Karis, it was just a matter of putting her in several situations that tested her character and, ultimately,**

caused her to rethink what it means to be true to that good heart within.

Q: Karis's mother still seems to be reeling from the experience of having been a teenage mother, but her father doesn't seem to be as affected. Can you explain this phenomenon?

A: I think that there has always been a double standard when it comes to teens and pregnancy. More often than not, the girl suffers a greater degree of social stigma than the boy. While Karis's father certainly wouldn't want Karis to become pregnant as a teen, the sting of being a teenage parent was not as powerful for him as it was for Karis's mother.

Q: As a mother yourself, to what extent could you relate to the experiences of Karis's mother, as she struggles with her daughter's adolescent rebellion?

A: The older my kids get, the more I can relate to Karis's mother and the more I appreciate my own mother. My daughter, in particular, really makes me think and rethink what it means to rely on God's guidance for parenting. More and more, I have to say to myself, "Okay—we taught her well. Now it's time to let her put those lessons into action." In releasing some of the control, I find myself relying all the more on God's promises because I know that when I can't be there to watch her every move and whisper direction into her ear, He can.

Q: How do you hope that readers of your work who are not religious will respond to the portions of the book that examine faith and belief?

A: I hope that those portions will cause them to reflect on their values and beliefs. I hope that readers will think about how developing a personal relationship with God can provide even greater direction in life.

Q: You've written both nonfiction and fiction; how do they differ, in terms of your writing process?
A: I find that writing nonfiction is easier for me because I already know what I'm going to write. However, I do not find it as enjoyable as writing fiction. Writing fiction is more difficult and even frustrating, at times, but I find it immensely enjoyable.

Q: To what extent do you see your own writing as a kind of ministry?
A: My writing is definitely a ministry. There are many people who won't pick up a Bible, but they will pick up a novel. They relate to the characters and envision how God can do for them what He does for the characters. Jesus understood this—that's why He told parables. I count it an honor to follow His example.

Q: Which contemporary fiction writers inspire you, and why?
A: I read a variety of fiction authors—Vanessa Miller, Sandra Cisneros, ReShonda Tate Billingsley, Khaled Hosseini, and Walter Dean Myers to name a few. I also read a lot of historical fiction and nonfiction.

Enhance Your Book Club

1. Karis Reed keeps a diary in which she addresses herself and makes sense of some of the events of her life. Do you keep

a diary? If so, go back and reread your entries from a time that was especially challenging in your life. How did you question your actions and the events you were dealing with? If you don't keep a diary, consider doing so for a week. How do you experience the act of reflecting on your life? What are some advantages of recording the moments in your life that have an impact on you? You may want to share diary entries with fellow book club members, to compare your experiences and writing styles.

2. Karis is committed to supporting Marlon and his colleagues while they are stationed overseas in Iraq. Have you ever considered corresponding with a serviceman or woman or volunteering to support your fellow Americans in our armed forces? To see what you can do, visit www.uso.org/ for suggestions and ideas on how to lend your support to people serving in the military. Your book club may want to consider "adopting" a troop or unit and sending them care packages and notes of encouragement.

3. In *Trouble in My Way*, Karis finds a prayer for protection that she distributes to her friends and uses in praying for Marlon, who is headed to Iraq. Did you know that prayers are an essential component of virtually all religious traditions? Are there any prayers that you know or that you say regularly? When your group gathers to discuss the novel, share any prayers that you know, and learn more about the kinds of prayers that are familiar to your fellow book club members. You may want to exchange written prayers with each group member on an individual basis.

Want more teen fiction fun? Check out these titles: